# TRUE GHOST
# STORIES AND
# HAUNTINGS

Novels by Barb Shadow

*A Step into Darkness*
*Shifting to Black*
*Invitation to Darkness*
*Touched by Darkness*

Poetry Collections

*Among the Dying Violets*

# TRUE GHOST STORIES AND HAUNTINGS

Barb Shadow

From the Shadows Publishing
Forestburgh, New York

TO THE THINGS THAT GO BUMP IN THE NIGHT, WITHOUT WHOM
NONE OF THIS IS POSSIBLE.

# CONTENTS

# HAVE YOU EVER SEEN A GHOST?
# ...OR MET UP WITH SOMETHING REALLY TERRIFYING?

As a paranormal investigator and author of a series of horror novels, these questions are posed to me quite often. The answer to the first is yes. Yes, I have. And the second is, well, a little touchier. What's your definition of *really* terrifying?

I've had encounters with the unexplained for most of my life. When I was ten years old my grandfather passed away and I would lie awake at night listening to the house settle. In the quiet dark of my bedroom, he'd talk to me. I never mentioned it to anyone as it seemed perfectly natural. Other things, though, weren't.

Each night, I'd turn off my light and commence a running leap into bed. My feet were always tucked tightly under the sheets, and I slept against the wall, as if that would shield me from ghosts and monsters. Every creak of the floorboards would leave me statue still, breath held, waiting to hear if something ghoulish was coming closer.

Yet I was the kid drawn to cemeteries and tales of the dead. Abandoned places. My nightstand held creepy books and I sought out every Bela Lugosi, Boris Karloff and Vincent Price movie I could find. Christopher Lee. Lon Chaney, Jr. Every Hammer film. If I could find a movie or book about ghosts or something crawling out of the depths of hell, even better. Saturday afternoons were spent in my grandmother's bedroom, glued to her nine-inch black and white TV, searching for episodes of Creature Features, The Outer Limits and The Twilight Zone.

I became fascinated with psychic phenomena, premonitions and precognition. Clairvoyance. Every little "odd" occurrence in my day-to-day life made me ponder. I'd rest our old Webster's Dictionary, the kind with the Bible paper pages, on its spine and focus on a page number. More often than not, the book would fall open to that page or very close to it. Influenced by the way I held it? Probably. I was a child, after all. But this was my beginning. My intent was there. And intent can move mountains.

By the mid-1980s I had begun keeping a journal of my paranormal experiences. I'd note dreams that seemed exceptionally vivid, objects that went missing and were later found in strange places, appliances that turned on with no one around and the toys that were played with in the attic when no one had access. And more. Some experiences were comforting while others left me shaken, questioning reality and existence. I wanted answers.

Eventually, I co-founded the Sullivan Paranormal Society, an investigative team in upstate New York. Calls came in from museums, libraries, private residences, theaters and historical societies. We did walkthroughs of cemeteries and researched local folklore. "Ghost-lore." I continued my personal journal while separately filling notebooks with the details of our investigations. Audio and video recordings permeated my laptop.

For years, I tossed around the idea of publishing my experiences, but something nagged at me. This was only one person's story. The ghostly realm surrounds us all, and more people have encounters with the unexplained than not. I wanted to tell those stories. Show others that this is more normal than paranormal. Tell the experiences of people who are dealing with this other realm every day, yet you'd never know it…because brushes with the unexplained are often too personal, too taboo, to discuss. In my travels, I've even met a few seasoned investigators who prefaced their personal experiences with, "You may think I'm crazy, but…"

I can assure you, I don't. And the majority of people I've spoken with need that reassurance. That they haven't lost their minds. That they aren't alone. And, for some, that they can get through it. Hopefully this book will help. Nearly 150 personal stories from people like you, along with a few of my own, are featured here.

Have I ever seen a ghost? Yes. Have I ever crossed paths with something *really* terrifying? Perhaps you should turn the pages and find out. — *Barb Shadow*

# 1

# DID YOU SEE THAT?

Apparitions. Ghosts, spirits, wraiths, shades. Who hasn't found themselves sitting around a campfire, listening to tales of phantom hitchhikers, a lady in white crossing a cemetery or a faceless shadow appearing on a bridge at midnight? Who hasn't retold the story of the train, speeding toward a cliff, saved at the last moment by a mysterious flagman who then faded into the shadows? And who hasn't, as a child, stood transfixed before a bathroom mirror, chanting, "Bloody Mary, Bloody Mary…" in nervous anticipation of a gruesome specter appearing?

We've all heard stories of encounters with the dead, but what happens when those legends are exchanged for reality? When the people involved are credible and it isn't just a campfire tale? From my experience, the first reaction is disbelief. "It must've been a shadow. A trick of the light." Yet something shivers at your core and the subject is changed.

The first time I encountered an apparition was on a crisp fall night in 1997. There was a bite of frost in the air and I was cozy in bed, enjoying the quiet of the house. My children were asleep. I rolled onto my right side, and something told me to open my eyes. There, in the darkness, stood a woman.

I held my breath and stared. I'll never forget what I saw standing just three feet away. The dress was old-fashioned with a high neckline, long sleeves, and a row of buttons down the sepia material. But there was no body. No head, hands. No face. So close I could have reached out and... I was under the covers like a shot, gripping them as if my life depended on it. When I finally got up the nerve to peek, the woman was gone. I laid there for the longest time, wondering what, or who, I had just seen. And why.

I mentioned that night to my mother years later. Ghosts weren't a subject we generally spoke about. She supported my interest in the paranormal and occasionally asked about my investigations with the team, but it wasn't her cup of tea. As I described the minute details of the dress, Mom's eyes got wide, and she left the room. She returned with a photo of my grandmother, her mother, taken in 1917 on her wedding day.

"There's no denying who was at your bedside," she said.

There in the photo was the exact dress I had seen, and I had never been shown that picture before. In sepia, the way my grandmother had chosen to appear. Why she showed up without her body, I'll never know.

In 2006, in the same house, I heard my seven-year-old son rouse in the night. I peered through the darkness and saw him waiting in my doorway, his shadow illuminated by the clock in the living room.

"Coming, honey."

As I approached him, I reached out to touch his back to guide him back to his room.

He wasn't there.

Startled, I walked down the hallway to his bedroom. My son was in his bed, asleep, and the figure I had seen was gone.

Although I've seen my share of shadow figures, my most recent and unique "run in" with an apparition occurred in February 2022. Driving home from a trip to Pennsylvania, my boyfriend and I turned onto the road adjacent to his, a few minutes from his house. It was dark, about 7:30 p.m., and we were ready to get home, put our feet up and have a glass of wine when something dashed across the road in front of the car... right in the headlights. It was tall and person-shaped, a "solid" white mist. We pulled over.

"Did you see that?!" My boyfriend is a skeptic and a member of Sullivan Paranormal but there was no debunking what had run in front of us. Had it been human, we would have hit it. But no person could move that fast. It was too cold for fog (and fog doesn't run across the road), and there were no vents of any kind where steam might emanate (but, again, this was a "body," not a cloud of any type). We sat for a minute or two, stunned at what we'd witnessed. "Should we go back and come through again?" he asked.

"Hell, yes!"

Darren turned the car around and we rolled through the area once more, catching sight of the same figure on the opposite side of the road. It darted toward the bushes and was gone. We continued slowly to his house and later returned to try to get it on video. Nothing. In the weeks since, we have confirmed that there had been a car accident very close to our sighting of that apparition. One person was killed.

Apparitions are much more common than most people believe. About a year before my mother passed away, she was hospitalized and spent a week in the ICU. She'd been sedated and told me that during that time she witnessed deceased relatives pass by her window. Some she hadn't thought about in many years. At first, she was concerned they had come to take her, cross her over, as if they worked for the Grim Reaper himself. I believe they were watching over her, knowing her time left on earth was short, and were waiting to greet her when she decided to let go.

I'm sure my mother never mentioned her "sighting" to anyone else. Those who have crossed paths with the departed often remain silent, rarely discussing their experiences with more than a trusted few. Or none. Of those who submitted their personal experiences to this project, most were excited to share their encounters. Some asked for advice. A few, however, desired anonymity. They were willing to talk about what they had seen but were nervous about having it in print. They were afraid of disbelief and ridicule. Hopefully the following accounts will help break that stigma.

## The Wedding Band

Sixty-three years ago, I lived in a haunted chateau in Orleans, France. Every night a spirit woman would visit and play with me. She especially loved playing on the staircase and always went downstairs during our playtime. I asked the owner, in broken French, if she knew who the woman was, and Madame Aubert told me it sounded like her mother who lost her wedding ring before she died. One day my mother was cleaning the fireplace in the living room and found a gold band under the slate. I told her about my spirit friend and what Madame Aubert had told me. I asked Mom to put the ring on a table so she could find it. That night my friend came to visit, and I told her we found her ring. We played for a bit, she went downstairs, and when she returned, she kissed my forehead, smiled, and disappeared through my shuttered bedroom window. The next morning the ring was gone, and she never returned, but I was extremely happy for her.
– *Debra M., Florida*

## Let the Sisters Sleep

Years ago, I was employed at a convent, located in Lemont, as a nursing manager. My duties included covering for the midnight nurse if she got ill. Anyway, on one night I had to go in at 3:00 a.m. A nursing assistant and I were the only ones on the infirmary floor. At the time there were sixty nuns on the floor.

As I was heading to my office, I saw a nun at the end of the unit dressed in her habit. The only thing I was thinking was that only myself and the aide were on the floor. I was worried that this nun would wake up the other sisters, so I started to approach her and said, "Hey, Sister, what are you doing up? Go back to bed. Everything is okay." I kept walking toward her and talking to her. She didn't respond. Then it hit me that no one on that side could get up without total assistance.

I stopped in my tracks while she kept walking toward me. I saw as she approached that she had no face or feet. I didn't think I could run as fast as I did into my office, and I slammed the door. The aide then knocked, came in and said, "Oh, you saw her, didn't you?" She then told me that she saw her all the time. – *Maura C.*

## His Final Moments

My dad passed away unexpectedly on April 24, 2012. I never got to say goodbye. We went to his funeral. Afterward, we went back to my dad's house with his wife, and I remember a wave of calm coming over me. I remember getting off the couch and walking outside down a small path to his shed. I looked up at the sky and the clouds started to darken. I then looked over at his shed and saw my dad walking out of it. He was wearing his brown and white striped dress shirt he liked to work in, his khaki shorts and khaki shoes. He looked over at me as he was walking out. He stared at me for a few seconds before kneeling down where his lawn mower was. Then, he disappeared.

I remember standing there for a few seconds before turning around and going inside. When I got back inside, I sat down and his wife asked me, "Do you know what time it is?"

I said, "No, why?"

She looked at me with a mix of confusion and shock on her face. "It's 7:45 p.m." I stared at her, and she said, "This is what time your dad died."

I blinked and said, "I didn't know that." Then I told her what I saw.

She turned white. "That's what your dad was wearing when he died."

That's how I knew what exactly happened to him. He showed me his last moments on Earth. – *Megan B., Ohio*

## An Era Long Gone

I have lived in the Eureka Springs, Arkansas, area for over forty years. In the early 90s, the famous Crescent Hotel closed. A friend I worked with rode with me, and we stopped at the hotel so he could talk to his wife. She was looking after affairs for the owners. As we entered, we both glanced into the dining room that was immediately to our right. We saw two couples dressed in Victorian clothes sitting at a far table near the window.

We quickly walked away to find his wife thinking the couples were actors for some commercial, since Eureka Springs is famous for that era. We found his wife in a side office and asked about the couples in the dining room. She said nobody was supposed to be in there. The three of us went into the dining room. There was no one there, but two chandeliers were swinging back and forth in unison in about a three-foot arc. – *Victor B.*

## Unfinished Business

2005 – I was working security at "the Baird building," a two-story business on Baird in Midland, Texas. I had to walk the halls, making sure everything was secure, three times a night. On this particular night, I was walking the second floor. I had just come around the corner and was surprised that a man was in the hallway. He came from an open door and had his head down looking at some papers he was holding out in front of him. I assumed he was an employee who had stayed late due to some legal things that needed addressing, and walked toward him, calling, "Hey. You're not supposed to be in here!"

I vaguely recall his legs not really ending in feet. He wore jeans and a blue, long-sleeve, button-down shirt with the sleeves rolled up. He was towheaded and never made a move to acknowledge that he'd heard me. I reached the point where I was sure he'd walked into another office on the opposite side of the hallway, only… it was a wall…

I never went back, even though I needed that job. – *Julia C., Texas*

## She Wore Flannel

One night, my husband was upstairs in our bathroom when he called to me and asked me if I just walked into our bedroom. I told him no, that I was still downstairs. He said he swore that he saw a woman wearing a flannel nightgown walk into our room. First of all, I don't wear flannel. Lol! – *Edna W., New York*

## I See You

I grew up in a haunted house that had a couple of ghosts. One was a little girl everyone but me had seen at some point. Aside from the few things that would fly off the shelves or walls, or the TV and radio going crazy, or something waking me up by sitting on my bed every night, that was all I had experienced…until one day after school.

My sister and I were the only ones home. I was thirteen and she was sixteen. I was doing the dishes. In front of the sink was a big window. Now, my sister had a thing about always trying to sneak up and scare me. It never worked and drove her nuts. So, I was washing the dishes and looked up. In the reflection of the glass, I thought I saw my sister sneaking up on me. I started to laugh and called her a dope. I said, "I see you. You can't scare me."

Well, as I said this, she literally floated to my side. We ended up shoulder to shoulder. At this point it still didn't register that it wasn't my sister. We turned and looked at each other and, again, I said, "I see you."

That's when I saw her face.

Big blue-gray eyes, long ringlets of brown hair and a look of shock at what I had said. She flew off in a gray-black mass into the next room. That's when I knew it wasn't my sister. That was the first and last time I saw her plain as day. I think I scared her more!
– *Tara C.*

## Little Girl Ghost

I went on a tour of the old Tooele hospital in Utah. While sitting in the lobby hearing its history, I looked across the hall at a door with a foggy window and saw a short shadow walk past. When the tour started, I learned that the door led to the nursery and that they have a resident little girl ghost. – *Rory O.*

## A Message for Mom

I have been able to sense spirit and see apparitions for as long as I can remember. The house we currently live in is inhabited by two children, a boy and a girl. Right after buying the home and redoing every room in the house, we moved our family in. I was awoken by the laughter of children and at that time our son was seventeen and my grandmother was in her room upstairs.

I walked into what is our dining room, but what I visualized was a living room with furnishings from the 60s. The children were playing in the middle of the floor and apologized for waking me. I asked if they were okay, and they said they were fine and asked me questions about who we were – how exactly our family unit worked and if it would be okay if they stayed till their mother came for them. I said that was fine, introduced them to my dog who had been very aware of them, and went back to bed.

Time went by and I came home from work one day to my grandmother and the lady from whom we bought the house sitting on the porch. She had brought us some fudge and was looking at all the changes we had done to the home. She stayed for dinner and said her husband would be wondering where she was. I walked her out and as she passed the two trees on either side of our walk, she paused. It was the moment it was revealed to me that she was the mother of the children I had seen. I touched her hand and said, "Mrs. C-, your children are fine, and they are waiting on you."

She immediately wrapped her arms around my neck and hugged me, sobbing. To make a long story short, she was the mother of eight children, all born in this house, and two had died here – the boy and girl. A tree was planted for each child beside the walk. I had never known any of this but, as I said, this has been ongoing with me. – *Holdon T.*

## A Man and His Dog

I lived in a house in Newark, New York. It was haunted by a man and a black dog. I would see the dog come up from the basement and walk right past me into the bedroom. The house was over a hundred years old. Sometimes, I would hear the dog growling by the bed while I was sleeping. – *Maxi D.*

## And Then He Was Gone

Sitting in my apartment at 11 o'clock at night, watching the news all alone…to my left is the archway to the dining room and beyond that is the kitchen. I had a light on in my living room where I was and suddenly there was movement to the left of my eye. I froze.

I thought, "Oh, my God, somebody's in the apartment with me," and I really didn't know what to do. I sat in silence, waiting to see the figure once more.

It went by again, a small, dark figure…very fast…but seemed it was a little slower than the first time. I finally got the courage up to turn my head and look and watch. I saw nothing. Turned back again to watch the news and it returned, but it only came out and peaked at me from around the corner of the dining room. It was a little boy with dark hair, maybe five years old, and he had on an old-time housecoat, the old worn plaid ones with the ribbon around the edges… and he smiled.

And then he was gone, and then he was gone, and then he was gone. I was stunned. – *Gail D., North Carolina*

## Once a Prankster…

I lived in a house about thirteen years ago in the area called Twin Aire, that was established during the 1950s. It was a one-story house, and my husband and I moved in with our two sons so we could have a bigger home.

Shortly after we moved in, I was sitting in my bedroom, on my bed. The mattress was on the floor. This bedroom, the smaller of the two, had old fashioned closet doors that were hard to open. In order to open the door, you had to turn the handle, lift up and pull hard. All of a sudden, the door opened and slammed into my bed.

I sat in shock, staring at the now open closet door. Needless to say, I got up and walked out of the room. I stopped outside the door and stood there, watching. After a few moments, I decided to go check on the laundry, which was located in the room at the back of the house. At this time, my oldest son was also using it as his bedroom because he wanted his own space away from his younger brother. I walked into this room and was about to open the washer door when I heard a noise in the kitchen. It sounded like a chair being moved.

I checked and saw all four chairs were in their places. After changing over the clothes, I went into the kitchen where I saw a dark shadow standing in the doorway between the kitchen and the front room. I stood, rooted to the spot, staring in shock. It disappeared and I backed into the room, then hurried toward the back door when I heard a man laughing. I rushed outside into the yard.

After what seemed like forever, but was probably only about twenty or thirty minutes, I decided to be somewhat brave and went into the house very slowly. I saw and heard nothing until later that evening.

My husband and youngest son were sitting at the kitchen table eating supper and talking when something flew by and hit the bottom of the table. We looked and saw the gold angel with the suction cup on its back that I always stuck to the bathroom mirror of whatever house or apartment we lived in. It was laying on the floor. We sat there, shocked, because there was no logical reason for it to have landed where it did. If it had fallen on its own, it would have hit the sink and landed in the bathroom, which was located off the kitchen. We then heard a man laughing from the bedroom my husband and I shared and saw a dark shadow walk into the room.

We lived there about three more months and, fortunately, in those three months nothing more happened. The only explanation I can think of is, about a week after the incident, a family came and asked to set up a small vial of a cross, flowers and candles in our backyard. The woman explained that they had lived there before us, and her son had been shot in the backyard and died before help could come. I told her what we had been experiencing and she said it must be her son. He had been a jokester. I asked her to please ask him to stop and invited her inside. She spoke to him and asked him to stop playing jokes on us and scaring us. Amazingly enough, I guess he listened because we didn't have any more issues at that house. – *Athena S., Indiana*

# The Lady in Black... and More

Like many people, I grew up not believing in ghosts, spirits, or the paranormal. I watched the movie Poltergeist with amusement and not fear. I appreciated all the work that went into creating the special effects to try to make it seem real.

All that changed in January of 1997.

I was driving home from work at about 7:30 p.m. in a light snow. There was about an inch on the ground, and it was still falling, so I turned off the radio so I could hear my tires on the pavement and concentrate on the road conditions. One of our local streets runs parallel to a former railroad, which is now a bike trail. It goes down a hill, and at the bottom it intersects with a street from the right that passes under the trail. That street has a guardrail on the far side because it also has a stream that runs alongside it, which goes under the street I was on.

As I drove down the hill, I saw a woman on the other side of the cross street walk out from under the trail trestle, right next to the guardrail. She stopped at the intersection and looked in my direction. I turned on my right blinker and started the turn. As my lights crossed her body, I looked at her face and she was looking across her left shoulder directly at me. Her body was as solid as anyone I'd seen. I finished my turn and started for the trestle when my brain realized she didn't belong. She was wearing a long, black dress that looked like it belonged in the 1800s. She was wearing a small hat with a sort-of veil that just covered her neck. Her hands were in front of her, and a purse hung from her left elbow. There was no snow at all on her clothes.

I slammed on my brakes and skidded to a stop, looked over my shoulder, and backed up. She was gone. There was no trace of her. No footprints in the new snow. No indication she was ever there.

Shaken, I drove the last four blocks home and parked in the garage. I walked through the kitchen and into the living room to hang up my coat. My wife, noticing that I was visibly shaken, asked with a concerned smile, "Are you okay? You look like you've seen a ghost."

I replied, flatly, "I think I did."

Her smile vanished. I proceeded to tell her what had just happened. We both agreed that we were not going to tell anyone about it, for fear that people would think we were nuts.

For three years it remained our secret.

In January of 2000, our house became active. From then until approximately 2010 we had several paranormal experiences. All of them except one occurred between the months of October and March.

It started one night after we tucked in our girls, ages five, two, and two. In the bathroom, between the double sinks and the mirror were two wall-mounted toothbrush holders with glasses. The girls' toothbrushes were all too big to fit in the holders, so we just laid them on top of the holes on either side of the glasses. We'd had ice cream after dinner, so I brushed the girls' teeth to make sure they were done well. Upon finishing, I laid the toothbrushes down where they belonged; the youngest's on the left side of the left glass because she was left-handed, the middle child's brush on the right side of the left cup because she was the middle child, and the eldest's brush on the left side of the right glass. We tucked them all in at about 8:30 p.m. and climbed into our own bed to watch television. Our bedroom was at the end of the hallway, and from there we could look all the way down the hallway; the stairs leading down to the right just outside our door, then the laundry behind bifolds on the left, the youngest's room on the right, the bathroom on the left, then the middle child's door on the left beyond the bathroom, and finally our eldest's room at the other end of the hall around a small jog in the hall.

We watched TV with a small lamp alight on the small table next to my wife's side of the bed. About 9:15 p.m. we heard a noise from down the hall as if something had fallen into one of the sinks. I looked in on each of the girls and all of them were sound asleep. I walked into the bathroom to discover the youngest's toothbrush, which had been on the left side of the left glass, sitting in the right-hand sink, about two feet from where it had been placed. I spent the next five minutes trying to drop the toothbrush from where it had been and seeing how it could end up in the right-hand sink. It would have had to make it around the glass to end up in the right-hand sink. I walked back into our room and explained to my wife what I had found. We chalked it up to some weird bounce that I couldn't replicate and went to sleep.

A few weeks later we were once again watching TV in bed in the evening. Around the same time of the night, two lotion bottles and a picture frame flew off the side table and landed on the floor about ten feet away, skidding to a stop near the bedroom door. It was as if someone just swiped their arm across the table but didn't touch the lamp. It scared the hell out of both of us. Fortunately, none of our girls were awoken by the noise. We put things back where they belonged.

The following year we had another paranormal experience around dinner time. Two of our girls were helping set the kitchen table and our oldest was helping cook. I had gotten home from work, changed clothes, and was walking through the living room towards the kitchen when a plastic headband that was sitting on the library table behind our couch flew off the table and onto the floor just as I walked past it. The noise startled everyone and our girls who had been setting the table were shaken because I was still five feet from the table!

Two years passed without incident until early in November of 2002. We were in the middle of remodeling the first floor of our house. We had ripped up all the flooring, so it was nothing but subfloor everywhere. The girls were in school, my wife was at work, and I was in the basement beneath our foyer working on a laptop with our family cat at my feet. At about 10:30 a.m. I was startled by the sound of dress shoe steps from above. I sat and listened as they came from the left (the far end of our living room), went right over my head, and through our coat closet! I ran upstairs and there was no one there. Our doors were all still closed and locked.

In January of 2003 I was in Utah on business assisting with a software upgrade for a client, our girls were in school, and my wife was home doing laundry. She had dumped the clean laundry onto our bed and was folding it when she heard the clanking of glass bottles behind her. She turned around to find a round perfume bottle partly tipped and leaning against another round bottle. We never had mice in that house, so to see something like this "just happen" scared my wife to the point of calling me in the middle of the day and telling me what had happened. I did my best to reassure her, which was only moderately successful.

The house seemed to calm down after that until July of 2007. We had arrived home from a vacation a few hours prior to this incident and I walked upstairs to go to the bathroom and change the laundry around. I got to the top of the stairs and turned right to go past the laundry to the bathroom. As I walked past the laundry area, I looked at the far end of the hallway where a large collage of pictures hung in a frame. In the reflection of the glass, I could see the hallway walls and myself walking towards it. Just before I got to my youngest's room, in the reflection of the glass I saw a shadow pass across the wall across from her room, but there was NO shadow on the actual wall itself. It was only visible in the reflection and disappeared.

After this last experience, our paranormal activity ceased. When we sold our house and downsized in 2018, I was relieved to NOT see "paranormal experiences" on the house condition report!

But here's a little background to our story...

The small Wisconsin village where we lived was a bustling community back in the 1800s due largely to the number of lead mines in the area. At one time our little burg was bigger than Milwaukee! Because of American Indian hostilities in the area, in 1832 the U.S. Government built a fort just south of the village for the townspeople to live in during that summer. It was unused after that summer and eventually disappeared from the landscape. When the railroad selected this village to build a depot, people from the adjoining town started moving and that community all but dried up. Several buildings, including their stagecoach stop, were moved from there to the village where we lived.

During the time we lived there I dedicated ten years to my community, serving on the village board, as Village President, and on several committees. Each year all of us on the boards and committees got together for an end-of-year celebration. It was during one of these evenings I started talking with a man I'll call Stan, who I had become friends with over the years. Stan was living in the former stagecoach that had been moved to our community and turned into a private residence. I cautiously danced around the topic of the paranormal, eventually asking if he'd experienced anything of the sort. He confided in me that there were several evenings when he'd be watching TV and a man in 1800s garb, complete with prairie hat, would appear at the top of the stairs and start to walk down, and would disappear before reaching the bottom. All the while, a woman he described as "a painted lady" would watch from the top of the stairs. I told him a few of the things we had experienced.

The evening ended and we each headed home. I found out later that on the way home Stan told his wife about what I'd told him and then, for the first time, he told her about the man and woman he had seen off and on for years. She replied with, "Well, did you tell him about the little girl?" He then learned that from time to time his wife would wake up during the night to find a little girl, about eight years old, standing at the foot of their bed just looking at them. Then she would disappear. Until then, they had both been experiencing things but never told each other about them.

When my wife was in college, she became friends with a woman named Julie who lived about thirty miles away from us. The two became best friends and Julie moved into our second bedroom so she could work at a local company, whose business is VERY busy in the fall, and didn't have to drive back home late at night after her shift. During that time, we learned that when Julie was twelve years old her sixteen-year-old sister was killed in a car accident. She confided in us that after her sister was killed, Julie was able to see and communicate with spirits of the deceased who hadn't yet crossed over. Not believing in anything of the sort at the time, I listened with skepticism and curiosity. I wondered how an intelligent person like her could believe in something like that.

After college graduation we kept in contact with Julie and we visited each other from time to time as our schedules allowed, but never discussed the paranormal with her. Even after my full body apparition sighting, we didn't talk with her about it. Once we had had several paranormal events in our house, we decided it was time to invite Julie over to see what (if anything) she could tell us about what she sensed. We invited her to spend a day with us, not telling her about anything paranormal.

Once Julie had arrived, I revealed to her that we'd had some paranormal experiences and would like to know what she could tell us about certain areas we would be visiting. She smiled at my wife and said, "Oh, like the short woman sitting next to you on the couch?" We saw no one. She then went on to describe a spirit who bore a striking resemblance to my wife's paternal grandmother who had passed away in 2010 and who, during her life, was known to be a practical joker. We smiled at each other and then Julie and I got into our car to visit some of the areas where things had happened. I pulled over to the side of the road on the hill above where I'd seen the apparition. I asked her what she sensed. She told me she saw a young woman, maybe in her thirties, standing at the intersection. She wore a dress from the 1800s, a hat with a short veil in the back, her hands in a muffler in front of her (the kind used to keep hands warm during the winter), and a purse over her left elbow. She said that she had been a teacher in a school up the road and was walking home when she was struck at this intersection by a horse and buggy and died of her wounds. She felt that the woman's name was Miss Victoria.

Even though we'd told her nothing of my experience, she was able to describe the woman to a tee, even seeing the muffler that I hadn't noticed. We also hadn't told her that just up the road behind where Miss Victoria had appeared there was an old school building that had been converted into a residence.

Next, we drove a couple blocks away and parked across the street from Stan's house. She looked at it for a couple of seconds and said, "I see a man in a prairie hat at the top of the stairs, a painted lady behind him, and a small girl." Only then did I tell her what Stan and his wife had been experiencing. I was quite surprised at her ability to see things that no one had told her.

Sadly, Julie passed away in 2017 following a brief illness.

One other experience which eluded me when I wrote up everything else, was that of a dark figure. One night while my wife slept, I laid in bed beside her, watching TV. During a commercial break, I muted the sound as I always have. Just then a VERY tall figure, probably seven feet tall, appeared next to my wife's side of the bed towards her feet. All I could see was a black shape without form, similar to how the Grim Reaper is shown. It slowly leaned slightly over the bed, turned its "head" towards my wife's face, and then vanished. Even though she woke up a few minutes later and asked me to turn off the TV, I didn't tell her about the figure until the next morning. She was somewhat shaken by what I told her, but not enough to affect her ability to sleep soundly on subsequent nights.

In 2010 (?) we engaged NIPIS (Northern Illinois Paranormal Investigation Society) to do an investigation of our house and the immediate area. They arrived during the afternoon to walk through the house, get electromagnetic (EM) readings, and discuss our experiences with them. They also left behind an EM meter on the dresser where the perfume bottles had moved. The meter recorded some elevated levels throughout the night, despite there being no electrical wiring nearby.

They also came back that evening and walked around our yard, down the bike trail behind our house, and over the trestle where the full body apparition had appeared.

During their investigation they took many readings and pictures. Most of what they took pictures of didn't result in anything abnormal, with the exception of a series of three pictures taken thirty seconds apart. They were standing on the bike trail directly behind our house and took them facing west in the direction of the trestle. The investigators say that during that ninety second interval a mist appeared from their right (the direction of our house), crossed the trail, and disappeared to their left. The first picture shows a small amount of mist on the right side of the frame. The last one shows the mist on the left side. The middle picture shows what appears to be the rough outline of the bottom of a skirt and legs.

After these pictures were taken, the team walked to the beginning of the trestle. One by one each team member crossed the trestle while people at both ends took pictures. The pictures didn't reveal anything, but when one woman was about halfway across, she arched her back and screamed in pain, then ran the rest of the way across to her teammates. She said that something scratched her. There were no marks on her shirt, but when it was lifted, they saw a very fresh scratch just below her horizontal bra strap. It was about four inches long and was about one-half inch wide at one end and tapered to a point. When the team presented the report to us about seven weeks later, they told us about what happened to her and said that the scratch was just beginning to heal, which is much longer than it normally takes. - *Alan D., Wisconsin*

## Out of Place

Although it happened over twenty years ago, I remember it as if it were yesterday. I was working for a large telecom company in their computer facility in Alpharetta, Georgia. At the time, I worked the graveyard shift in what was referred to as the "Tape Pool." The job required me to place tapes in the computer drives, to either label the tapes or input information, and then remove the tapes and replace them in the tape library when finished. That's what I was doing when my encounter happened.

As there were only two of us on the complex, we had to take turns for our lunch break. My coworker had just left for her lunch break, and I started to sweep the drives of tapes on our UNIX machines. As the machines were short, about the height of a dishwasher, I had my head down pulling the tapes from the drive slots located on the front of the computers. Once I grabbed as many tapes as I could, I started to turn and head to the library to place the tapes in their racks. When I looked up there was a man standing in front of me. He stood about 5'8", had black slicked-back hair, was clean shaven, and was wearing a white tee shirt and overalls. He looked to be in his early forties and stout of build. The thing that really got me at the time was the look on his face. It was the saddest expression I had ever seen.

Then, he was gone.

I blinked and he was no longer standing in front of me. He just disappeared. Needless to say, I was shaken.

Once my coworker returned and my lunch time was next, I went to my supervisor and asked if he had heard of anyone that may have died in the construction of the building or while working there when the computers were installed. He informed me that if there had been a death, he hadn't heard of it. I told him of my experience, and he said I wasn't the only one who mentioned seeing strange things in the building. This was the only paranormal experience I've ever had. I've not heard or seen anything like it since, and I'm fine with that. – *Darrell S., Georgia*

## A Warning in the Night

In my childhood home, we had a few odd things happen but the main one was when we had gone to a drive-in theater. It had snowed a bit by the time we got home, and being young, I had fallen asleep on the ride. They carried me into the house. In the middle of the night, they heard a loud *bang bang bang* on the side of the mobile home but there were only two sets of tracks outside. We got a call the next morning to call my grandma on my dad's side. She had passed away in the night. A month later the same thing happened, *bang bang bang,* and a call saying to contact Grandpa. He had passed in the night. – *Kim S., Michigan*

## Adam is Mad

I'm writing to tell you about two experiences I've had with my child. The first happened when she was about four years old. I was sitting on the floor in my living room, putting hooks in Christmas decorations to hang on the Christmas tree and my daughter had her back to me, drawing and coloring, as she hummed to herself.

Some movement caught my eye, coming up on my right side, so I turned my head and looked up, expecting to see my boyfriend. Nobody was there. Now this confused me, because I swore I saw somebody walk up to me; so I turned my head, thinking he walked behind me and was rushing to the bathroom. As I turned my head, out of the corner of my eye, I saw this shadow continue to dash past me and up the stairs. I shrugged it off, thinking I was imagining things and went back to getting ornaments ready. My daughter stopped coloring, turned around and said, "Adam is mad at you. You saw him and didn't say hi."

Now this gave me serious chills, but I just apologized and said hello to Adam. I told my boyfriend about this once he settled after work. We decided to do some research and discovered the house we were living in was part of what used to be a big farm. When tuberculosis was raging rampant, it killed a little boy who lived here. His name was Adam. Talk about instant chills! We even went and found his and his family's tombstones in the old cemetery at the end of our lane. – *Shannon L.   *Experience #2, "In the Company of Angels," can be found in Chapter 5.**

# Little Boy on the Stairs

Even as members of a paranormal team, we have experienced some paranormal activity in our own house. It was definitely more active when our daughters still lived at home. Both daughters are sensitive, but my younger daughter Cari is a ghost magnet, a beacon for spirits, especially those needing validation.

On one Saturday afternoon, I left the house with my two then-teen daughters and their friends to visit one of our local museums. (Yes, I had teens who actually enjoyed museums . . . especially if they were haunted!) We left my husband Steve at home by himself except for our nine-year-old dog, Meisha. Steve was in the kitchen next to the stairs that led down to the basement. This was also Meisha's favorite hangout, as this was a central location where she could see into the kitchen or living room, down the hallway to the bedrooms, or down the stairs into the family room. So, there was Meisha at the top of the stairs teasing for a belly rub.

As Steve was giving Meisha a belly rub, he happened to glance down the steps and saw a little boy looking up at him. The boy was about four or five years old. He had blond hair and was wearing a blue shirt, black pants and suspenders. This little boy was smiling at Steve, and waving to him. Steve was very surprised. He had seen a white lady apparition in our upstairs hallway before, as well as girl apparitions in a haunted asylum about an hour and a half away where we used to investigate a lot, but this was the first time he had seen a color apparition.

Steve quickly ran into the office to grab my camera to take pix, but the boy was gone when he returned. He then ran to our bedroom to grab his new CellSensor EMF detector and took it down the stairs to the spot where he had seen the boy. The needle went off the gauge in this area and the alarm went off. When he received the EMF detector from his devoted and loving wife for Christmas, he had done baseline readings in our house, taking it around the whole house to see what kind of readings he got in different areas. In that landing at the bottom of the stairs, the testing had shown that the needle had barely moved.

Besides seeing the little boy apparition, Steve also saw a shadow person about halfway across the family room in the basement, rising up from behind the loveseat that sat perpendicular to the stairwell to the main floor. The shadow person was also gone when he returned with the meter.

He immediately called my thirteen-year-old daughter (our "ghost magnet") on her cell phone to ask her to describe the little boy she had seen on the same set of stairs a different day, one who had been peeking up at her in the living room. The descriptions matched! Next came trying to find out who the little boy was and why he was in our house.

This little boy was subsequently seen other times in our home, both by Steve and Cari. Cari is a sensitive who sees spirits on a daily basis, which includes her twin brother Cade. This may be part of the reason why she is so connected with the spirit world. My husband Steve is more sensitive than I am, but not as sensitive as Cari. My older daughter Alyssa is very much a skeptic who has her own share of interesting paranormal experiences but has the definite opinion that not every experience is paranormal. Alyssa keeps us grounded whenever we go ghost hunting at other locations.

One summer evening the four of us gathered together in the family room in our basement to communicate with Cade. We call this our "family circle." Steve was seated on a loveseat, which faced our open laundry room door. I began to notice that he kept glancing curiously into the laundry room from time to time. (The laundry room and the storage room beyond it was the epicenter of paranormal activity in our house.)

At first Steve didn't say why, until he finally told us that he had been seeing a spirit in the darkness of that room. The spirit had finally been curious enough to move forward into the partial light at the door, and Steve was able to see that it was the same little boy he had seen on the stairs. Cari could see him too, confirming what Steve was experiencing. My "spirit" son Cade told us, through his telepathic link with his twin Cari, that the little boy's name was Jordan. Jordan was four years old and had died in 1885. Jordan was shy, which was why he wouldn't join us in the family room. Also, it broke my mommy heartstrings when I learned through Cari and Cade that Jordan was searching for his mommy and daddy. Poor little Jordan had been searching for so long.

I spoke quietly to Jordan and invited him to join us in the family room. I reassured him that we were just talking together as a family and would welcome his company. Even with all of the encouragement, he hesitated near the door and wouldn't come out.

I told Jordan I knew he was looking for his mom and dad and wanted to be with them again. I told him that if he sees a bright light - the brightest light ever - and walks towards that light, he will find his parents. Steve and Cari said Jordan disappeared soon after.

A few months later, with no further contact with Jordan, Cari, Alyssa, and I found ourselves in the family room with two of their very close friends, once again communicating with our Cade. Cari told us that Cade was sitting on the floor near the door to the main floor, petting our dog, Meisha. Alyssa had to go to the bathroom and opened up that same door, closing it shut after her.

Cari told us that Alyssa had walked through Cade. I looked over to that spot with a moment of melancholy, wishing that I too could see my son. I was feeling sad about it but wasn't ready for the hugely overwhelming feeling of sadness I felt, so much sadness that I was fighting the tears, trying hard not to sob uncontrollably.

I turned back to the three teen girls and saw they had odd expressions on their faces. "Suddenly, I felt like crying," I told them, having difficulty explaining through the emotion I was feeling.

"So do we!" they said, and we all began weeping – an out and out crying jag.

When I was finally able to talk a few minutes later, I said, "I don't know why this is happening, why we all feel like crying."

Cari came over to sit close beside me. "Mom," she said.

"Cade told me that Jordan just crossed over."

Jordan was finally with his mom and dad.  <3

About six months after Jordan crossed over, we attended a paranormal event where two psychics had been hired to give readings. I had a reading with Karyn Reece of Williamsville, NY, near Buffalo. After I sat down at a table across from Karyn, she looked behind me at about waist level. "Who is Jordan?" she asked me. "There is a little boy following you named Jordan. He has blond hair and is about five years old."

I was almost in tears. "Jordan was a spirit in our home. We helped him cross over to be with his parents. Why is he here?" I was fearful that Jordan wasn't with his mother and father.

"He did cross over to be with his parents," Karyn assured me. "But he can visit. He comes to your house because he likes the family atmosphere there. If you ever hear bouncing balls, that is Jordan. Jordan loves balls!"

I was so glad to hear that Jordan had really found his parents and could indeed come back to visit us. – *Tamora L. Vang, New York*

## In the Rocking Chair

I had an encounter with a female spirit in an old house on the square of Crown Point, Indiana. The house was about 200 years old.

She was so beautiful!! And looked very old at the same time. I was taken by her beauty; I wasn't afraid. It was broad daylight, and she was rocking in the rocking chair in the room. Her clothing was beautiful and old fashioned. I felt calm.

Then, she looked at me and said the most horrible words to me. Excuse the language, but she looked at me and said, "Get the f*** out of my house!"

I was mesmerized by her beauty and shocked by her words. My natural reaction was to ask her, "What did you say to me?!"

She repeated it!

I backed out slowly and didn't come home until another roommate returned. He called a friend who lived there once and said, "Tell Diana what you experienced." It was identical!

The lady I can only assume was the owner of the house. The house is still there. It's an historical site that will never be torn down. – *Diana H., Indiana*

## We're Out of Here

My friend and I were driving through San Francisco at twilight. We decided that we were going to drive around the Presidio cemetery. We were looking at all the graves as it was getting darker. Up in the back where the oldest graves are, we both saw a white, see-through figure...a male wearing ragged clothing and walking on our right down a row of headstones.

My friend said, "Stop the car! I want to go after it!"

I said, "No, no, we're out of here!" I drove out of that cemetery as quickly as I could. – *Gina A., Washington*

## A Ghost at the Stove

Years ago, I met a girl and she invited me to her house. I went there a few times. She was a smoker and would stand by her kitchen stove and turn on the exhaust vent to take out the cigarette smoke. One night while we were watching movies, I went to use the bathroom. The house was dark except for the light over the range hood of the stove. When I came out of the bathroom and started walking down the hall, I had a clear view into the kitchen. I saw a girl standing by the stove. I couldn't really make out any features, all I could see was long straight hair, like the girl I was there visiting. There was a counter with cabinets over the top that you could see through, so I could only see her from the waist up.

When I got back to the doorway of the bedroom, I said playfully, "Hey, what are you doing out there?" …talking to the person in the kitchen.

"Who are you talking to?"

I turned and saw the girl sitting in the bedroom. When I looked back at the kitchen, there was nobody there. My body immediately got goosebumps.

I looked back at her, and she said, "You look like you just saw a ghost."

"What the hell is going on here? There was somebody standing in your kitchen!"

I had some other minor experiences in the house, so I knew there was something going on, but to actually admit that I saw a half-body apparition and know that I actually saw it, was a pretty cool experience that I will always remember. – *Darren S., New York*

## The Shadow at the End of the Hall

Late September 2011. It was 6:00 a.m. and my alarm was going off for work. I got up and walked quietly through the living room to the kitchen to put on a pot of coffee. My wife had fallen asleep on the couch in the living room the night before. I hadn't disturbed her.

Before I could get to the kitchen, though, I noticed in the darkness of the hallway, a woman kind of going back and forth between our children's bedroom doors. I watched her for a minute, then whispered, "What are you doing?"

"What?"

I jumped as the voice came from beside me and saw my wife, still on the couch. I told her, "I saw someone. A woman. She stood, swaying, between the kids' doorways. I thought it was you!" I looked back down the hallway. The figure was gone.

It hadn't been her.

I've always been a skeptic and examined the hallway from every angle to see if it could have been a trick of the light, or if I could recreate the shadow that I thought was my wife. I couldn't. – *Liam O., New York*

## Pickett's Charge

So, here is one story with my daughter. To the best of my knowledge this is true. My daughter had never been to Gettysburg, let alone on a ghost tour. The day of the ghost tour, I took her to the battlefield. Specifically, the area of Pickett's Charge. We got out of the car and started to walk up the path that leads out into the field. As we walked, we passed a statue and a plaque. I didn't look at them then. My daughter felt nauseous, had stomach cramps and in general was in a lot of pain.

We walked out to the platform, and she insisted she saw men laying in the field. I did not. She pointed and said, "Daddy, there are men laying there." I just couldn't see them. Then, we started back. In the same spot, she had the same feeling she had going up. This time I did stop and look at the plaque. She had those experiences around the same spot that General Robert E. Lee met his men coming back in retreat. Did Robert E. Lee reach through the ages to touch my daughter? I think he did.

Also involving my daughter was the Jenny Wade house. There was a legend that if a single lady put her ring finger through the bullet hole in the door, she would find the person she was going to marry within a year. Well, my daughter did that. We thought nothing of it.

Flash forward a year later. I won't go into personal things here, but my daughter and my ex ended up in Florida. There, my daughter met a man who soon called me to ask for my permission to marry her. Of course, I said yes. This isn't as cool as the previous experience, however, did Jenny Wade help my daughter find someone? Does Jenny Wade help young ladies find love because her life was cut short? Possibly. Here is the caveat for this one. My daughter had stomach pains in the house, and they subsided once we left. She said to me, "Daddy, I think Jenny Wade might have been pregnant." I said I didn't know. I've since found out. I think she was.

Shortly after my daughter was married, she called to tell me she was pregnant. Was Jenny Wade pregnant? I don't know, but it makes for a good story. – *John F.*

## Keeping Watch

I've seen things all of my life. One night I drove a friend home from work. When I pulled in, I saw his neighbor looking out of a dark window. I mentioned that she must be wondering who was in his driveway.

"Who?"

"The elderly lady next door wearing glasses."

He got quiet, then said, "She died yesterday. There's no one in that house." He even got up early the next day to verify no one was there. That was the first time I was validated. – *Margaret M., New York*

## The Old Lady Sitting Right There

My sister bought an old house. It might have originally been a bed & breakfast, I'm not sure, but she later turned it into one. My wife, daughter and I moved into the house, and, for a while, we ran the B&B.

My daughter was three or four years old at the time and would know things before they happened. Little things. She'd tell me to answer the phone before it had a chance to ring, things like that. One time she told me, "Grammy's here."

I looked outside and told her no one was there.

She said, "Grammy's here."

Five minutes later, my mother arrived at our house.

But, one day, she was in her room playing and I heard her having a conversation with someone. I walked into her room, and she was alone at her Little Tyke's table.

"Who are you talking to?" I asked.

"That old lady."

"What old lady?"

"That old lady sitting right there." She pointed to the other side of her table.

Was there an old lady sitting there that I couldn't see? I think so. – *Darren S., New York*

## Baby

About eight years ago, my husband and I came home to find four hunters in our house. They were all dressed in camouflage with blaze orange vests or hats. One of them spoke to me. Three of them were sitting on the couch with a large dog that looked like a Dalmatian. They told me they were going hunting for the weekend and would I please take care of their dog. I said yes. They thanked me and disappeared.

The next morning, I opened the front door and there was what looked like a large Dalmatian dog. I said to my husband, "I told you!" It turned out to be a Blue Tick Hound. I kept her for a week, waiting for the hunters to somehow come back. I was calling her Baby. Eventually, I took her to the vet. She was chipped! We found out the original owner was deceased, and the son who owned her now was deceased, too! We also found out that the father and son were both killed in hunting accidents and the dog's name was Baby! – *Cynthia L., Michigan*

# Timeless Love

I met my husband-to-be right after he came home from serving in the army in Vietnam. This high school girl was struck by the handsome soldier, and we dated until I graduated and then got married. For forty-three years, raising two kids, we had such a happy marriage. He was the love of my life and my best friend. He lost his battle with bladder cancer (which was due to heavy exposure to Agent Orange while in the jungles of Vietnam) and I went into a state of depression without him. His last words to me were to promise to still try to sell our house and move closer to our daughter – to build a house on the land we had purchased. He wanted the reassurance that my daughter and her husband would be near me, and I wouldn't live alone, as our house was far away from other relatives.

Three weeks after he passed, a knock came to my door. It was a local man asking if my house was still for sale. We had listed it but had taken it off the market when my husband had gotten sick years before. Did Hank send this man there? A relative of the man wanted to move to our area and I agreed to sell the house. I moved to a rental down the road from where my new house would be built come spring. This is where I really became sad – I had heard of stories where someone who died would come back to "visit" and now that I was staying in this strange house, I thought the chances of that happening would be gone.

One night, I was sound asleep and woke up to a warm feeling. I opened my eyes to see my husband standing over me, next to the side of the bed. He looked perfect, young and handsome like the day we met. Not in pain or with his one arm folded and hanging awkwardly (due to the stroke he'd had). He stood tall and youthful and in a blue V-neck sweatshirt and jeans. I just stared at him. Could it be a dream? BUT then he bent down and kissed my lips and said, "Incredible," and smiled at me. Then he was gone. I've never seen him again, but know he was with me and was proud that I fulfilled my promise to him to build my new little house near our daughter.

It made me feel better to know he is okay and not crippled or in pain any longer. I miss him so much but now I know he is in a better place, and I thank God for allowing us one more visit. After that day, I started feeling better inside and started focusing on the house being built and our new granddaughter who was born just four months before Hank died. I hope he visited my daughter's house and saw his granddaughter. I think he did as when she started talking and saw the photos of Hank on my bookshelf, she would walk over to them and say she knew him. – *Kathy S., New York*

## A Boy

About nine years ago, I went back home to Indiana to visit my family. My son was a year old at the time. I was changing him upstairs in his room and he kept pointing off to the side. I asked what it was, and he said, "A boy."

Well, when I was two, my brother (nine) was hit and killed by a drunk driver. I'm assuming it was him. This wasn't the only time someone mentioned a boy in the house I grew up in. – *Sarah F., Indiana*

## Surrounded

The experience that sticks out the most happened when I was a child. I was five when it started. We lived in a neighborhood called Cherokee Village. I know the Cherokee once lived there because finding arrowheads was common. We would find them in a field beside the creek. I lived across the street.

Every night when I went to bed, color "dots" came out. They were beautiful and I loved them. I played in them, tried catching them. But the dots would leave and when they did, the ghosts started coming out of the closet, surrounding my bed. I was so scared. I slept with the covers over my head every night. There were so many, all staring at me. It happened for years until we moved. My older sister shared a room with me but she never saw a thing. I think back now, and I don't know how she didn't, but she didn't. I loved the dots, looked forward to them. I had told my mom, but she didn't listen. I wanted one of the dots to prove it. Every time I caught one, it would be gone when I got up. I can remember the dots as though it was yesterday and I'm fifty-nine. They were such a joy.

I wish I had looked at the ghosts more. I can remember a very old lady and a tall man. They always came out first. There were so many. I had two older brothers, but I was the only one that saw them.

When I was in high school, I went to a slumber party. I about fell over when we got to the girl's house. It was the same house where I had experienced all the ghosts. Not saying a word, I spent the night. She had my brother's old room. I didn't see anything this time. – *Mardonna F., Tennessee*

## A Grandfather's Love

I was a very young child when my grandfather passed away in Poland. My parents packed their bags and headed out the door to catch the first flight. I was crying in bed when I felt someone sit on the edge of my bed. I lifted my head and there he was...I knew it couldn't be as we already received the news of his passing, but there he was. I slid closer to him, and I felt him wrap his arm around my shoulder. He whispered, "Don't cry. I will always be right here." I looked up at him, we smiled at each other, and, in the blink of an eye, he was gone. – *Patrycja W., New York*

## Everything in its Place

Back when I was around four years of age, we moved into a new house that was built by our neighbor's father. I'd wake up at night and watch a man wearing khakis with a brown belt and a tucked-in, light blue, collared shirt, carry a box down the hallway into my room, and he'd put it up in my closet. My closet had access to the attic storage. I had this encounter many times. Also, when my bed was positioned so I could see down the hallway, I watched scary faces, heads only, popping out from the wall where the dining room was. They were black but had several colors covering over the face like you just saw a flash of light.

Later, when I was older, I was at my neighbor's and saw a photo of her father and recognized him as the man I always saw carrying the boxes into my room. – *Rebecca A., New York*

## At the Bedroom Door

I've lived in a few [haunted houses] but most memorable was the one with the little girl. My daughter described her as having long black hair, dark eyes, and bruises. I would hear a knock on my bedroom door and, "Mom, open the door." No one would be there, and I was usually home alone. We moved out and the next family didn't last long, either. Don't even get me started on the basement…

The basement was like walking into a room of people with no one there. The kids wouldn't go down there. We found a room that looked like it was used a long time ago to hold someone against their will. You would get pushed going up the stairs. It was just a horrible feeling. You weren't alone.

My youngest feared that house. She kept saying the little girl came to see her at night and she followed my oldest around. At first, of course, I didn't believe them…until the door knocking and calling me mom. Then I was like, "Okay, there may be more to this little girl thing, after all." She would run past my husband. He would think it was one of our girls, go into the room he saw her run into, and no one would be there. – *April H. K.*

## Great Grandma's Visit and Lady's Passing

I'll tell you of two experiences as a child that got me to eventually explore haunted places. First, I was six years old sitting on my bed, talking to my great-grandmother. It was a very comfortable and fun conversation and a bit odd, especially later when I told my mom about the encounter. She informed me that Great-Grandmother Malone passed away almost twenty years before. I described her to a "T," including the mole on her right cheek. I thought it was cool. Mom…not so much.

My second experience was in second grade. My school was three blocks away so, more often than not, I would walk home for lunch. It was raining pretty hard, and I went to the side entry where I took off my boots and coat and patted the family dog, Lady. She was wet, too; I remember very specifically. As I opened the door to the main house, I saw my dad was home and, looking at him, I saw something was wrong. He told me he just got back from the vet where they had just put Lady down (old age). I told him he was wrong and that I just petted her, and she was behind the door. My dad was cool, so he said, "Let's take a look." We did and there was no Lady. There was, however, a wet fur smell that lingered for days. Dad said, "I think that was Lady saying goodbye." I've seen and experienced hundreds of happenings since then. – *Mont S.*


## Expect the Unexpected

Shortly after we bought our house in Dover, PA, I was standing in the kitchen and, plain as day, the form of a man just walked right past me, through the wall and everything! At this point in my life, all I could say was, "Well, then, I should have expected that!" …Our house was built in 1840… - *Cari F.*

## Shadow Visitors

I live in a very old house in South Carolina. I moved back home after fifteen years of being away. During that time my grandpa had gotten sick, and my grandmother was in the first stages of dementia. I was taking care of them both. Many strange things happened. One time, I was sitting in a chair in my grandmother's room in the dark, which I did a lot. I would sometimes even sleep in the chair. That way I could hear my grandfather on his monitor. That night I was praying, and I had a weird feeling someone was watching. When I opened my eyes, all I could see was a dark face inches from mine, mouth open as if yelling. There have been other times when I saw shadow figures out of the corner of my eye and a few times I saw a dark shadow sitting on the end of my dad's bed.

Before my grandfather passed away, he would stare over the top of his bedroom window. When his hospice nurse asked what he was looking at, he said he was watching the kids play (a glimpse of heaven is our explanation).

A few people have told me they have seen a man pacing back and forth on the front porch. Sometimes I can see a shadow walk past my bedroom window. There was another time I woke up and there was a girl standing over my bed. I thought I was dreaming at first but blinked and wiped my eyes and she was gone. – *Jessica K., South Carolina*

## Now, Don't Forget

March 2014. I was at my oldest daughter's house in Florida. Our friend was in the Mayo Clinic, and they had given her only days to live. On Sunday (before she died), I was reading the morning paper in my daughter's kitchen around 6:00 a.m. Out of the corner of my left eye, I saw someone walking toward the kitchen, looking for something . . . a woman wearing a white shirt and light blue shorts with dark hair. I leaned back to see if anyone would go out the front door. No one was there!

My daughter and husband woke about half an hour after I saw the woman and I knew it wasn't either of them. The woman I saw was shorter than my family. I told my daughter what happened. Trac knows I seem to experience things.

We went to the Mayo Clinic that afternoon and Annet wanted to know why Trac was there to see her again. Trac told her we hadn't been there earlier. Annet insisted that we were. She said, "I saw y'all this morning!" My daughter looked at me, nodded, and smiled. This was who I saw that morning. She was looking for her son because he was to stay at my daughter's house overnight.

I have a friend who is scared of the paranormal but loves to hear people talk about it. Many years after this happened, I told her about some of my experiences, but not this one having to do with Annet. As I was waking up the next morning, Annet appeared to me and said, "Don't forget to tell them what happened between you and me." Annet was wearing a red, short-sleeve polo shirt, black shorts and was younger looking. Oh, I did tell my friend about it the next time I saw her. – *Jane K.*

## The Gray Man

When I was a small child, two or three years old, my family had to move in with my grandma. She lived in a house that had been built in the late 1800s and there were a lot of places where the floor would squeak when someone walked. I was asleep but woke when I heard the floor squeak. I looked to see who was walking into the room and saw a tall man. He was grayish with dark spots for eyes. As I watched him, he started to walk toward me. I screamed and he disappeared.

When my mom came to me, she asked me to describe the man. After I told her, she said it sounded like her father, who loved kids and wouldn't hurt me. I wasn't so sure since as I didn't think he looked very friendly. He appeared the next night and the night following. Mom started to leave a nightlight on for me. It didn't stop him from coming into my room, but he didn't seem as solid, so I was able to sleep. I had several experiences while living in that house but the first one will always be a standout for me. – *Constance M., Indiana*

## An Angel or...

I saw a white shadowed man outside of my sister's house last year. I was the only person awake. He walked around the house and vanished, then came out the other side and vanished again. I saw him disappearing, heading for the barn and, again, coming out of the other side. My two brothers-in-law got killed in an accident two months earlier. I don't know if it was an angel or the spirit of a man that died in a trailer down the road. – *Maxi D.*

## Grandma's Goodbye

My experience with the paranormal came over the course of my forty-one years of life. When I was around ten years old, I would sleep on my aunt's couch in her living room. Up until one night. I was seeing weird lights, a twinkle of a sort, and then they would disappear. The next night I tried again, thinking it was my imagination. My grandmother had just passed from pneumonia, and I swear I saw an image of her in front of me that night. I never slept on the couch again! – *Christina M., Pennsylvania*

## Still in Charge

Back in the summer of 2000, I was a corrections officer for the Louisiana Department of Corrections at Louisiana State

Penitentiary at Angola, the largest maximum-security prison in the U.S., as far as land mass goes.

One night, I was falling asleep in my chair. As I started to nod off, I got this feeling to look toward the walkway door. I looked and saw a Freeman (slang for corrections officer) standing there. He was a tall, skinny guy, young looking, with a thick mustache and dark hair. I saw the gold on his collar, so I knew he had rank (a lieutenant or higher). He knife-hand pointed at me and did the "come here" wiggle. I thought I was getting fired for sleeping on the job. I walked the ten to fifteen feet around my security desk and looked back at the door. There was no one there.

Now at night, the Key Sergeant (guys who let you and inmates in and out of the dorm) opens and closes the heavy steel door. Loudly. I walked past the game room into the TV room (where the door is) and didn't see a thing. Two inmates were watching TV, but both were short or average size guys. I asked them if they had seen a Freeman here just now and they said, "Sarge, I don't know what you're smoking, but I want some."

I said, "Man, if it makes me see stuff, you can have it." I turned and started walking back to my desk when the door opened, and it was my captain making his rounds.

I thought nothing of it and finished my shift. A year later, I was working at a different prison and told a coworker about it. He said it sounded like Captain David C. Knapps who was killed December 1999 at Camp D where I had been working. I didn't think anything about it until almost two years later when I was working at Angola again and saw a picture of Captain Knapps. I'll kiss your tail if that wasn't who I saw. I figure he saved my job, too. A captain seeing a fresh cadet falling asleep, gotta wake him up.

2003. I was a corrections officer at Angola once more. I was working the same dorm, Falcon 3. It was about 3:00 a.m. All inmates were asleep, and the TV was off. All quiet. I was nodding off again. Something told me to look toward the walkway door. I looked up and saw a tall guy, standard inmate uniform of white shirt and blue jeans. He walked from the TV room into the game room. I never heard the door open or close, so I figured maybe the Key Sergeant was security scenario-ing me. I got up and walked around the ten-to-fifteen-foot desk to see who this inmate was, because if you come into the dorm at night, you go straight to the desk. So, I went into the game room to chew ass, but nobody was there. I scratched my head and started making a round. One inmate was awake, shining his boots. Short guy, nicknamed Bravo. He asked me, "See a ghost, Sarge?"

I said, "Maybe."

"What'd he look like?"

I described what I saw, and Bravo said, "Oh, that was Hightower. He died here two years ago."

He said it so nonchalant it threw me for a loop.

2003. Same dorm. 3:00 a.m. Nodding off. All the inmates were asleep. I got the feeling to look up at the game room this time. Between the bathroom and game room there's a cinder block wall just big enough for one man to lean against. Next to the water fountain was a "shadow man." Just a man made of pure shadow but with white eyes. He was sitting on the floor. We locked eyes and the shadow man stood up in one fluid motion, kind of flexing at me. I shook my head, and he was gone. To this day this one gives me the willies. From my understanding, I witnessed an entity known as a shade. Not a ghost but a manifestation of energy. – *John B.*

## You're Not Alone

Back in 1985, I bought an old house beside a river in Maine. It was built by a colonel who served in the American Revolution. The day my son and I moved in, he flatly refused to sleep in the room that my dad and I had fixed up for him and instead took his sleeping bag and slept in a small narrow room under the eaves.

On the first weekend that I was alone in the house, I was in the shower and the water suddenly went cold. I quickly got out and found the hot water to the bathroom sink running and splashing over the sides of the basin; it was flowing so hard. It had never run that fast at full capacity when I used it!

Items started disappearing over the next month or so and were eventually discovered in a suitcase in the downstairs closet. One morning, I was putting in my contact lenses and the saline bottle moved about six inches all by itself.

I had a party at my house one time. Most of the people attending exclaimed about how warm and welcoming the house was, but one of my coworkers was ill at ease and, after a short while, she said she had to leave. She later told me my house was haunted but would not elaborate.

I always felt that whatever was in the house was a protector and never felt threatened…only startled at times! We lived there for eighteen years, and odd little things happened occasionally just to remind us we weren't alone. – *Brenda W., Maine*

## Goodbyes

My grandfather visited me after his death. No speech. He was wearing the suit he wore at family gatherings and was smiling.

My next-door neighbor passed in the hospital. He visited me in his suit. He looked sadly at me and walked through the wall to his house. The next day his wife told me the news. I already knew but I couldn't tell her that I had seen him until years later.

When my niece was born, I was the caregiver. I was Uncle Michael and Aunt Michelle together. We'd be on the couch listening to the Dave Matthews Band. She was only a few months old. I was holding her and singing to her when a woman I didn't know appeared to be walking by the dining room. She didn't look at us. She just walked toward the outside. Your typical looking spirit, she was misty looking, like a white-ish ghost figure, wearing a white, almost see-through nightgown with blonde-colored hair and light complexion. She glided across the floor. This happened a second time shortly after, where she was walking up the steps. Same appearance. I actually stood up and watched her walk up the steps until she disappeared. – *Michael V., Pennsylvania*

# A Visit from Mom

Back in 2006, I moved to Texas to help care for my mom who was diagnosed with ALS. We usually spent the days watching TV together. One of our favorite shows was Ghost Hunters and I remember telling Mom how I believed in ghosts but never had any experiences. Mom just kind of gave me this weird look after I said that to her. She passed away the day after Christmas in 2006, and it was about six months later when things started happening around the house.

One Saturday morning, I was getting up about 6:00 a.m. to go check out yard sales around town. When I sat up in bed, about ready to stand up, I heard knocking on the wall in my bedroom. Just three raps as if someone was knocking on the door!

About a month later, I went out on the back patio for a smoke and, while I was standing there, I noticed my dog going crazy barking at something by the fence. He kept running back and forth by the rose garden. I thought it was maybe a cat up on the fence, but when I looked, there was this misty type of cloud hovering near the rose bushes. It was about 5:00 p.m. It was early summer and a nice day. This was not fog or dust.

I stared at the cloud while the dog ran around it, barking. It slowly dissipated after a few minutes and the dog stopped barking!

Then, a month after that, I went home from work and got on the computer in the den. No one else was home. It was quiet. No TV on. As I was typing along, I heard voices in the house, but they sounded like they were in the distance. The house had double-paned windows, so I knew it wasn't coming from outside. I just sat there at the computer, frozen, listening. The ALS affected Mom's throat muscles and her voice had gotten pretty raspy before she died. One of the voices sounded like her. I say ONE since there were two people talking! I couldn't make out what they were saying. It went on for a few minutes before they stopped. I moved out of the house shortly after, and Mom came with me to my new house! – *Mickey W., Texas*

## Testing the Bow

When I was a little kid, an old timer told us kids to look through windows and we would see ghosts. We looked every chance we had, and it finally happened. What we saw was a bow lift off the wall and the string pulled back like someone was testing it. It was then put back on the wall.

Another time, there was an old couple in their seventies, I would say. They were walking in a brushy spot going up a hill. I said, "Hi." They ignored me. Then, they walked right through the brush and disappeared. They looked as real as you and me until they started to disappear.

When I was older, I worked at the Hotel Jeffery, in the gold rush town known as Coulterville in California. Most of the ghosts there are friendly, but some are mean. One tried throwing me and my friend off the roof and another one always opened the doors for me when I had my hands full. Supposedly, a miner died in room twenty-two and isn't very nice to some people. A coworker left a toolbox in room twenty-two, and he went to urinate. When he came back, all the tools were scattered down the hallway. This happened numerous times over the years. – *Anthony B.*

# At the Foot of the Bed

We lived in a two-story house that was over one hundred years old in Wentzville, Missouri. I was nine years old at the time and was lying in bed. I couldn't sleep because my sister was snoring in the next bed. Our bedrooms didn't have doors, and I glanced into the hallway. Something was trying to take shape. It was white, but I could still see through it. I immediately put the covers over my head and, when I was brave enough, I lowered them. It was gone.

Years later I told my oldest sister about this experience. She said she saw the same thing, only it had the shape of an old woman in a long dress with her hair in a bun, standing at the foot of her bed. We had many experiences in that old house. – *Nena B., Missouri*

# A Prank Turned Ghostly

The place was Kimswick, Missouri. October 17, 2016.

My wife and brother-in-law were planning an event to scare my wife's sister. My brother-in-law arrived about five minutes ahead of us to hide so he could jump out from behind a large tree.

We had heard of people saying they would see ghosts walking in the cemetery at night, but I never gave it much thought. Our plan was to take photos with a camera and cell phones, then get close to the tree and have her brother jump out and they'd watch their sister run.

Our plan worked, and we got a huge laugh as their sister took off running just like in cartoons. Her feet were going a hundred miles an hour, but she wasn't moving.

About a week later, I uploaded the photos to my computer and what I saw shocked me. As I enlarged the photos, I saw one man walking south to north. He looked to be from the mid-1800s…much like Abraham Lincoln's time. Long tail in back, beard and high boots. Of the thirty photos I took, I was able to get what appears to be a young man walking and looking over his right shoulder as he is moving away. In another photo it appears to be the same person or spirit in front of me and I can see his chest…and what appears to be the same clothing worn in the previous photo.

My wife and I have had numerous events happen to us. I guess that is what happens when you look to share space or locations with spirits. We have doors that close in our home all the time. After my wife's father passed, we placed his guitar on a stand in the great room and would hear an occasional strum of the strings. Our friends freak out, but we just know it's spirit energy trying to communicate. – *Roy P.*

## That's Not My Brother

I always loved the paranormal but was skeptical that it was real before I had my experience, a little over a year ago. I decided to sleep with my bedroom door open, which I normally don't do as I fear the dark, but I wanted my cat, Penny, to be able to roam in and out as she pleased. The only light was the soft glow of my pink lava lamp.

I was lying in bed awake, trying to talk myself into sleeping when, for what felt like the longest split second, I saw my younger brother standing in my doorway. My heart then dropped and immediately I felt in danger and in a panic…and I'm not known for having panic attacks. What I saw I could swear on my grandmother's grave was real. It was him, but not.

I was so scared it might be a prank that I quickly went across the hall to find out if he was just at my door. Maybe I had been too tired to notice or hear him moving. But he told me he had been in bed the whole time and I woke him up.

I haven't slept with my door open since. – *Shaylyn B., Arizona*

# Thomas

I lived in a country town many years ago. My house ran along a forty-acre abandoned farm and we walked in the large field often. I discovered lots of perennial flowers. My friend and I, with our children in tow, decided to dig up some of the flowers to put in our gardens. My husband came with the tractor, and we loaded the flowers into the bucket.

On the way home, my dog began acting strange...barking at the air. We felt as if something was following us. The next morning, my oldest son told me he had gone to the bathroom in the night and had seen a boy around his age, eleven or twelve, looking in the window at him. The boy had brown hair, dark eyes and a white shirt with suspenders. My son said he put water on his face thinking it was his imagination but when he looked back at the window, the boy was still there. No matter how he moved, the boy stayed in the same spot looking in. Mind you, he would have to have been very tall, eight feet or so, to be able to look in.

Later that morning, my husband went out to work on the tractor. He spotted a young boy, eleven or twelve, wearing a white shirt, suspenders and brown pants. His hair was brown. As my husband approached the tractor, he asked the boy what he was doing. My husband looked down for a second and the boy was gone. The shear pins that held the brakes on the tractor had been pulled out and rested on the tractor.

Strange things continued to happen. My youngest son saw something in the upstairs window one night, twenty-five feet up. Something rode with me to work, an hour away, and a coworker picked up on the presence. My coworker told us she needed to leave as she felt that the presence was dangerous. I asked her to explain and told about the goings-on. I asked her what should I do?

I told her that a boy had come to my husband in a dream. The boy's name was Thomas Dudley. We explored the cemetery next to the abandoned farm and found his headstone. He was twelve when he died. My coworker said that because we took something from him, we needed to give something back. I placed a baseball on Thomas' grave. Sightings and experiences still occurred.

Shortly after, my husband had several affairs, and our marriage was falling apart. The friend that dug up the flowers with me was the one who told me of his second affair. The next day, she died in a motorcycle accident directly across the street from the abandoned home. I divorced my husband and left the area. – *Beth P.*

## A Final Goodbye and Forgiveness

I was an EMT and involved in a horrible car crash where a woman committed suicide by running head-on into the ambulance I was driving. She killed herself, and a six-year-old boy, instantly.

About two years later, I was sitting on my bed, writing down recipes, when I heard what I thought were my kids running across the kitchen floor to my doorway. I told them to stop running in the house and to go to bed. No response. I looked up and, standing in my doorway, was the little boy who was killed two years earlier. We stared at each other for several minutes until I got up to grab my phone. When I looked up, he was gone. – *Karen S., Oklahoma*

## Poppi

When my son was around two years old, he was playing in his room while I was in the kitchen. I heard him and thought he was talking to his toys. I went into his room and asked him who he was talking to. He said, "Poppi."

I never heard the name Poppi before that day. I asked him who Poppi was. My son got up, walked into the hallway and pointed to a picture on the wall. It was a picture of my (now ex) husband's father who passed away before I had a chance to meet him. When my son pointed to the picture, he said, "Poppi."

I called my ex-husband and told him what happened. He asked, "Are you sure he said Poppi?"

"Yes."

"Poppi is what my niece used to call my dad."

His niece was the only grandchild his dad ever met. – *Joana D., New York*

## 2

# DID YOU HEAR THAT?

While seeing an apparition – there one moment and gone the next – may be unnerving, hearing something unseen can be even more unhinging. Knowing something is in the room with you, possibly reading over your shoulder right now, or listening to footsteps slowly cross the floor... well, cue the goosebumps. Children's laughter when there's no one else home or a ghostly melody coming from an old piano make for a creepy story on a dark and stormy night, but what about when it happens in your own home? Spirits have ways of making their presence known and not all are comforting.

On an October day in 2007, I was home alone, sitting on my sofa, reading. The kids were at school, and I was having a quiet afternoon to myself. Out of nowhere, I heard steady footsteps coming up the basement stairs. There had been no thud of the basement door, and no one should have been coming home at that hour. I had just a moment to decide...sit there and see who walked in, or surprise whoever shouldn't be in my house. I gathered my courage and threw open the door, ready to confront whoever it was and protect my home. The stairs and the basement were empty.

It wasn't the last time someone, or something, otherworldly tried to come in. Less than a year later, one night in June of 2008, everyone was in bed asleep. My oldest daughter woke to hear the doorknob to the basement rattling as if someone was trying to open it. This went on for a few minutes, with pauses every so often. My daughter finally got out of bed and opened the door to see who it was. Again, no one was on the stairs. No one.

Fast forward to an evening in the fall of 2018. My daughter's boyfriend had just gone, and she and I were in the basement getting the laundry. We heard a knock on the door from the outside and shrugged at each other, figuring he forgot something and needed to be let in. She opened the door to… nothing. Her boyfriend's car was gone. Who has been trying to gain entry to my house?

Another time, my husband and I were sitting on the couch in our living room watching TV, while our middle child sat across from us using the computer. Our youngest was playing in his sister's bedroom while she sat in her doorway, texting.

BANG!!

It sounded as if something had slammed into our daughter's wall.

"Who threw the shoe?!" she yelled. "What the hell?!"

No one was anywhere near the hallway, and no one had thrown anything. My daughter said she felt a shoe whiz past her face and hit the wall. We searched… but nothing was found anywhere near her wall. No shoe, no nothing…yet we all heard it hit.

Something similar happened again in 2015. December 12, to be exact. I had run to my mother's house early that morning to help her with a few things. My husband and the kids were still asleep. When I returned, my husband told me he had been awakened by a thud. As if something had hit the wall and fallen.

There, on the floor beside his side of the bed, was our middle child's sneaker. Odd. My husband would have noticed it if it had been there the night before…and she never left her sneakers out, least of all in our bedroom. Add to that the fact that she was still asleep. So, tell me…who's throwing shoes? And why?

I believe something occasionally passes through this house and wants to be noticed. Perhaps it doesn't know any other way to get the attention of the living.

It would seem that spirits have different abilities in that regard. Many people report hearing their name called or a "Hello" when they are alone. After my husband passed away in 2017, I was in the bedroom gathering clothes to give to the funeral home. I had picked out a blue shirt and, as I held it, I clearly heard him say, "I like black." I paused, put the blue shirt away and took out a black one.

But the spirits can get even more creative than that....

## A Game of Pool, Anyone?

When I was five years old, we lived in a rental house. We didn't know anything about any of the prior tenants. This house had secrets we couldn't have imagined.

In the basement, there was a circle with symbols painted in it. My dad had tried several times painting over it, however, each and every time, the markings would bleed through. My dad ended up throwing a rug over it and placing our pool table on top of that. Little did we know we pissed something off and it would make its presence known.

One Saturday, my dad had to work and left. Mom, Heather (my sister), and I were at the house doing the normal things people do on a Saturday. My sister and I were in our room playing with our Barbie dolls and Mom was cooking dinner in the kitchen. All of a sudden, we heard our mom yelling at us, telling us to quit messing with the pool table. At first, I asked Heather, "Who is Mom yelling at?" because we were in our room. The second time she screamed at us to get our butts upstairs or we were going to get a spanking. I jumped up and ran from our room to let her know we weren't downstairs. When I got to the kitchen, my mom had the door open to the back landing that heads to the basement. I asked her, "Why are you mad at us?"

My mom turned white as a ghost and said, "Why were you

girls playing with the pool table?"

I told her we weren't, that we had been in our room playing with our Barbie dolls.

"Show me," Mom said. She grabbed my hand, and I led her to our room where Heather was still playing.

"See, Momma? We weren't downstairs."

My mom asked, "If you girls were in here all this time then who's downstairs?"

I shrugged my shoulders and told her I didn't know.

Mom started freaking out because she thought there was an intruder in our house. Mom and I went to her room, and she handed me a baseball bat and she grabbed Daddy's gun and back to the kitchen we went.

Now, we were really scared thinking someone broke into the house. When we entered the kitchen, we could still hear someone playing pool. The balls would crash into each other and then stop. Mom had me stand at the top of the landing with the baseball bat and told me, "Mandy, if anyone besides me comes up these stairs, you hit them as hard as you can."

I shook my head and said, "Yes, Momma." Here my mom was shaking like a leaf heading downstairs to confront whoever might be down there. Mom was yelling, "I am armed, and I will shoot you, so you better come out!" as she is turning all the lights on and searching the basement. She got to the pool table and found two pool sticks and balls scattered everywhere.

After a few minutes she headed back up the stairs. Mom asked me if I had seen anyone run past me. I shook my head no. Mom had us follow her back to her room to put the gun and baseball bat away. We were still scared since we didn't know if anyone else was in the house with us. Mom asked my sister and me to stay with her in the kitchen so she could keep an eye on us. Mom was back fixing dinner when we heard two sets of heavy footsteps run up the stairs and slam the heavy wooden back door.

The three of us jumped, screamed, and ran out of the kitchen.

Mom grabbed my sister and told her to lock herself in our room. Then, Mom and I went back into the kitchen to check things out. We opened the kitchen door that led to the landing, and we found that the wooden door we heard slam shut was still locked from the inside. The screen door was open and the gate to our fence in the backyard was open. I ran outside quickly to close the gate so our dog, Raffy, couldn't escape. Mom asked me to bring the dog in for protection and to go get my sister from our room. – *Amanda S., Kansas*

# Keep on Rockin'

I was little when I lived in Kansas. We lived in a white, two story, two-bathroom house where you could enter two ways into the front room. One was from the hallway that led from the front door and the other was from the kitchen that led from the back of the house.

My mom always played the piano at night while we kids (I am the youngest of five) took our baths and got ready for bed. One night after we took our baths, my three brothers, sister and I went running into the front room. We stopped in the doorway because there, in the corner, the rocking chair was rocking back and forth all by itself! Nobody was moving it. Nobody was sitting in it. No air was circulating around it! It was moving on its own.

My sister stood frozen behind me, and my two oldest brothers were in the other doorway. My youngest brother went running to our momma and hid under the piano bench where she was playing church songs. She turned and looked at us and put one finger on her lips.

"Shhh!"

She motioned for us to come to where she was, and we all ran to her. We kept watching the chair move while Momma played church song after church song and when she stopped playing, the rocking chair stopped moving! Momma said that it was a good spirit because a bad spirit wouldn't listen to church songs.

The next experience happened in Arkansas. It happened about a week after my dad passed away and all of us kids and my mom were finally home from the hospital, except for my sister. We lived in a house that you had to go through the front room and then the kitchen to get to the bathroom, and all the bedrooms were off to the side of the front room. Everybody was in bed except for my mom and me. We were in the bathroom. Out of nowhere, we heard what sounded like heavy footsteps that went from the front room to the kitchen and then back. My mom asked me if I heard it and I said, "Yes, Ma'am. Who is it, Momma?"

"It kinda sounded like your daddy's footsteps 'cause he always walked heavy and always wore cowboy boots!" And that is how the footsteps sounded when we heard them. We left the bathroom and checked on the other kids. They were all sound asleep. Nobody else was up.

The next one happened in Texas. My mom and I used to talk on the phone each day and one day we were talking about when it was our time to go, how would we let our loved ones know that we are gone? I told Momma, "Promise me that if you go before I do, don't scare me, 'cause I believe in ghosts, and I scare easily."

"I won't scare you, baby, 'cause I love you!" she said.

Then, one day, I got a phone call (my sister and I live in Arkansas) from my brothers that live in Texas where our mom and stepdad lived, that my mom was in the hospital and the doctors wanted all the family members there. My sister, my husband, and I went to Texas, and they put my mom in hospice. We stayed by her side with my brothers, my sister-in-law and my stepdad. While we kids were sitting around my mom, we knew that it was a matter of minutes because she wasn't responding to anything. My stepdad and my husband were in the waiting room. We kids were talking and singing my mom's favorite songs. Her door was open and, all of a sudden, it shut on its own! We all stopped and looked at each other. I asked everybody, "Did y'all see that?"

"Yes. Wonder what made that door close!"

I got up and opened it and asked my stepdad and husband if they closed the door. "No. We never got up. We thought that one of y'all did."

I told them, "No. We weren't anywhere close to the door." So, I checked it to see if it was easy to move on its own and I noticed how heavy the door was. There was no draft, either.

When I turned around, I heard my youngest brother say, "She's not breathing." And I went over to momma and checked her. I told my brother to go get the nurse because Momma was gone. That was my mom's way of keeping her promise to me by making her door close when she passed away and was leaving us. She did it that way so she wouldn't scare us because she loved us. – *Melanie M.*

## Tap, Tap, Tap

When I first moved in, I'm pretty sure there was a spirit already here. Within the first two weeks of being in the house, I heard a man clearing his throat. Then, on another day, one of my dog's squeaky toys squeaked in the living room as if someone stepped on it. My dog was locked in his kennel at the time. And then there was the time I heard tapping on a flat cookie pan that was in the drying rack in the sink – as if someone had flicked their finger up against it a couple of times. The faucet wasn't anywhere near it at the time, so there weren't any drips. – *Mickey W., Texas*

## A Visitor from the Past

I lived in a duplex many years ago when my daughter was little. This wasn't any duplex, it had been built for mafia mistresses as we lived halfway between New York City and Chicago. It was a perfect stopping point for the mafia in the 1920s. I lived upstairs and there was a set of exterior metal stairs leading to my apartment. Frequently at night, I would hear someone heavy climbing the metal stairs. I would peek out the front door, sure my neighbor was pranking me...but there was no one there.

The worst night of these experiences, I heard very heavy footsteps, the sound of the door opening and a very cold breeze in my living room. But the door never opened. I heard rustling in the kitchen, like someone preparing a meal, but there was no one there. This went on for several minutes. My daughter, who was in her room off the kitchen, began to cry. When I went to her, there was a very distinct black shadow at the foot of her bed. The shadow disappeared out her window. She refused to sleep in there after that and, within a few weeks, I found a new place to live!! – *Tina B., Tennessee*

## A Dire Warning

In 2001 I was visiting family in New York City. I was seeking out the usual tourist spots and was walking through, admiring, the World Trade Center. Beside my ear I distinctly heard, "Get out!" and felt an intense need to leave the building...and to get out of the city, to be honest. I left immediately, heading for home. Two weeks later, the towers were brought down.

Was this a ghost? A spirit guide? Guardian angel? Or perhaps a gut instinct? I may never know...but I will always listen. – *Anonymous*

## Time to Do the Dishes

Recently, my wife and I have had something turn our dishwasher on several times. It's only my wife and me in the house, so we don't use the dishwasher. But, about the same time, (1:00 a.m.), something has latched the door closed, turned the dial to heavy load and hit the start button on our dishwasher...pretty strange. – *Jerry W., Minnesota*

## Not the Rings

One of the more interesting stories I have is from when I used to live in a three-room house that was converted from an old illegal gambling place. Mobsters from Chicago would come down there to gamble. I would always hear a man and woman having a conversation and laughing. I couldn't make out what they were saying but always heard it.

One night, a friend of mine came over to spend the night. She took her rings off and laid them on my coffee table. The next morning, the rings were gone. We looked everywhere. Finally, and I don't know why, I looked in the trash can. About halfway down, under the trash, were the rings. We did not throw anything away during this time. No one else was in the house. There is no explanation as to how the rings had gotten into the trash. – *Sue W., Missouri*

## The Clock Chimed

For many years, my mother lived with me and my son. She had a fascination for the grandmother clock that stood in my living room adjacent to the front door. It was a beautiful clock, tall and stately, polished, yet it was a pain in the neck to keep running. It wouldn't work properly and no amount of adjusting the pendulums, winding, etc., would do it. My mother, however, loved the clock and would tinker with it whenever she could. It never worked for her.

I was home alone one afternoon, not long after my mother's passing. I don't remember what I was doing at the time, but I'll tell you, that clock chimed. It was wound and running, looking as perfect as the day it was delivered. I figured my son must've gotten it working and when he returned home from work later in the day, I asked him about it.

"I haven't touched the clock."

"What? You must have! It's running!"

He walked over to where the clock sat and looked it over. "I swear, I haven't touched this thing in months. It should be sitting there like a brick."

It wasn't. It didn't run for long and in all the years since it hasn't started up or chimed again. But I know it was my mother…making one last adjustment and, finally, getting the clock to chime. – *Marian O., New York*

## Apartment 1607

I used to live in a one-bedroom small apartment located in Katy, Texas. I was in a bad relationship. We fought all the time. I don't know if that anger and craziness stirred things up but the very first thing that happened was a coke can (half empty) tipped over and started rocking back and forth. We had no fans, no windows opened. We thought that was strange, but not too crazy, and moved on. A few nights later, we both were trying to sleep. There was a scratching noise (like nails under your pillow). I thought it was him. He thought it was me. After about two minutes, I yelled at him, "Can you stop!"

He replied with, "My hands are down here." They were resting between his legs. We both thought that was weird but went to sleep.

A few days later he was in the closet getting some clothes and a washcloth got thrown at him. I was in the living room watching TV. He came out looking white as a ghost! I've never seen him really scared before and he asked if I threw it at him and ran off. I laughed because I didn't and explained I was sitting down watching TV. There was no way I could have been fast enough to do that.

Skip to a couple of days later. I was home alone, trying to take a nap, and heard the scratching under my pillow AGAIN! I was honestly so tired I yelled, "Can you please STOP I'm trying to take a nap!" And it stopped. When I woke up, I realized, "Holy s***, this thing can understand me." Once it knew we knew it was there, the activity became nonstop. I never once felt threatened, though. We would try to sleep. Coins that were laying on the dresser, though, would get thrown around and hit the walls. The TV would get turned on every time we left. The back door would get unlocked - from the inside - after I locked it.

I think the scariest moment was when I was taking a shower. I felt a tap on my head. I honestly didn't think anything of it because at my mom's house, her showerhead was really low and I would bump my head on it sometimes but when I looked up and realized how far the shower head was from my head, I got scared. Then I heard a whisper.

"Jeeeessssicccca."

I said, "Hell, no!" and hopped right out of that shower! That shower always gave us the creeps. We used to wait in the bathroom for each other while the other one showered because it was that creepy.

One time, I was done cleaning the house and I had to take a shower with no one there because he was out doing something. When I got out of the shower, the word "hello" was written on the mirror. It was not his handwriting, and it definitely wasn't mine! Not to mention I just got done cleaning, so it hadn't been on there before.

Another time, I had a Maltipoo dog and I heard her barking in our room. I got up to look and she was growling and barking at a corner with nothing there. It frightened me, so I said, "Let's go!" and ran to the other room. I sat on the couch and when my dog jumped on my lap, she was SHAKING. Poor dog. I'd never seen her like that before.

At one point, we were recording a video (old-school phone but it did have video). When I was talking, you could CLEARLY hear a woman moaning loudly in the background. I can still remember exactly how she sounded, the pitch and everything. I could go on and on with crazy stories of the poltergeist activity that occurred in apartment 1607. But I am thankful for these events because once you ACTUALLY experience the unexplained and spirit world, you can never look at things the same again. My world changed for the better, and I saw things with opened eyes. I would love to go back and tell that ghost thank you. – *Jessica B., Colorado*

## Daddy's Car

This happened in Arkansas. I was nine years old when my daddy died in a car wreck and it seemed like everywhere that my mom and we five kids moved, the car was always there! There was this one time that we moved, and the car somehow got placed across the street in a field. One day, my sister and I, and our friends, were walking down the street when we heard, "Ginny Mae, come here!"

We all stopped because my sister's name is Virginia and only my dad called her "Ginny Mae." We looked around, didn't see anyone, and kept walking. Then, we heard again, "Ginny Mae, I said come here!!"

We stopped again and looked because it was in a stricter voice, and we saw that we were right next to the car that my daddy died in. We all screamed and went running into the house where my mom was. She asked what was wrong. We told her that we heard daddy in that car and explained what happened. Momma looked out the window and got on the phone. She sent that car to the crusher and had it crushed! – *Melanie M.*

## The Man

When my son was three or four, he would talk to someone he called "the man" every night in bed. We would tell him to stop talking and go to sleep. One Sunday morning while I was channel surfing, I came across a picture of Jesus on the TV. My son yelled out, "Look! It's the man!" – *Jerry W., Minnesota*

# "Hey" Man

I bought our old high school in Brodhead, Wisconsin, five years ago. It was built in 1906 and was in use as a school till it closed in 1996. It sat primarily empty till I bought it. The previous owners stripped the building of all usable materials and left us a mess to clean up. We wanted the old look for our haunted house business. Well, we got more than that. We found our building to contain multiple spirits.

As we started cleaning, we would find things that we thought were misplaced had been moved to other parts of the building. We also found when we set up our props in certain rooms, they were being played with. Yes, we were all skeptics, but when you're there all alone working you can feel a presence around you. You get goosebumps and your mood can change within a heartbeat. You always feel someone's there. I've had something come up over my shoulder and say, "Heyyyyy, what you doin'?" several times. We call him HEY. He has done this to several people who have attended the building or the haunt.

I also had several paranormal investigators come into the building with amazing results. The meters they used went off in various spots throughout the old building. Their Kinect cams showed stick figures trying to hide from them and some that interacted. The spirit boxes came alive with voices of children and adults alike. We have an old music room and when you sit in the silence of the building, you will hear faint singing of children coming from that area. We have had one of the spirits identify herself as a little girl about ten years old. Her name is Elizabeth. She loves to play games and interact with those she feels comfortable with. Elizabeth will light up the lights on Spirit Bears (trigger objects) that you tell her to. We have no known evil spirits that we've been able to detect. They are mostly peaceful or pranksters. The pranksters like to throw screws or nails at you. Not hard, but like a toss to get your attention.

One room on our third floor has beautiful wood beams supporting the ceiling. I have a video tape from when I first bought the building. In the video, those beams are pristine. No marks on them. But over the past couple of years, we are discovering handprints of little kids on them. They look like they are stained into the wood but after scraping some of them, the stain is only on the surface. If it was a real stain, it would go into the wood by several layers, but this is only on the surface.

We also have had, or we have taken, several pictures outside the building, looking in, and in the photos children or things appear in those photos in the windows. There are so many more experiences we have had, too many to describe. As far as we know, no one has died in the building. Everyone who attended this school, tells us that it was haunted back then and still is. We do know that the whole town has several Native American burial sites throughout and one of them was on our property. I love this old building and the experiences I have. I do let others come in and investigate and enjoy it with me, but never will I allow any Ouija boards or seances to be performed. Everything is good in there and we do not invite the evil or want to provoke anything ever. – *William W., Illinois*

## More than Just an Imaginary Friend

My husband and I bought a house that a childhood friend had grown up in. She had a brother who died from cancer just before they moved into the house. After having our son, we noticed him frequently talking and playing with an imaginary friend. I asked him some questions about his friend and got around to his name. When he told me, I about fell to the floor. It was Dean, the same as my friend's brother who had died. My son said Dean knew me from when I was a little girl. After that day, I also talked to Dean whenever my son did. – *Tracy D.*

# A Haunted Hotel

Last August, my daughter, Mikaela (twenty-seven years old), and I decided we needed a break and wanted a little vacation. I always wanted to visit Savannah, so we decided we would go there. I did a little research and, while I've always been interested in the paranormal, I've never had any experiences that were notable. I discovered The Marshall House, which is a beautiful Greek revival hotel built in 1851, smack dab in the downtown area. It was well known for the supposed paranormal activity that occurred throughout the halls. I thought, "Why not?" We booked our itinerary and headed for Georgia.

My daughter and I arrived and went to our room, number 423, which was at the very end of a long corridor with windows overlooking the dining area below. My phone was nearly dead from the drive, so I plugged it in to charge and told my daughter I was going to go out front to have a smoke. She said she wanted a shower, so off I went. I arrived back ten minutes or so later and discovered her standing near the door in her robe, wet hair in a towel. She stated that after her shower, while still in the bathroom, she heard a little girl's voice say, "Mommy?" It totally freaked her out and she tried calling me, only to discover I had left my phone. I thought, "Okay, no big deal," and we decided to do some exploring. I had purposely not looked too much into the exact paranormal activity because, if we had any, I wanted it to be without any predetermined thought.

We went to bed that evening and I was awakened during the night at the sound of a hard rubber ball being bounced on the floor next to my bed. When we went downstairs, I approached the Hotel Concierge and asked about the unusual sound and was told that, indeed, it was a common occurrence at the hotel. Well, we were surprised! I also asked where we might learn about some of the history surrounding the hotel. We were instructed to go to the second and third floors and walk the halls because there were photos hanging there, illustrating its history.

While strolling along reading about The Marshall House, my daughter and I were the only ones in the hallway. I heard someone say, "Hello." It was the loud voice of a young man, and it sounded as if he was directly behind me. I turned around expecting to find a person other than my daughter standing there. In fact, I blurted out, "Hi." We were alone in the hall. I asked if she heard it, and she asked me what I meant. She had not heard anything.

We went back downstairs to the concierge, and I told him of my experience.

"Oh, you've met the 'Hello Man,'" he said.

Wow! This was getting interesting!

Our final evening, we retired to bed only to be awakened at 3:00 a.m. I was startled by someone grabbing my hand and pulling. My daughter, on the other side of me, started asking, "Was that you? Did you do that?" Not knowing what she was asking me, I was pretty freaked out at the time, I also understood I needed to downplay the experience, or she would have insisted that we pack up and leave right that very moment. I assured her it was me.

I stayed awake reading the rest of the night. In the morning I told her about my experience, and she told me that at the same time I was jerked awake, someone was playing with her feet. She thought it was me.

I did additional research since we were leaving and found that the fourth floor was one of the more "active" areas. It was known for children playing, balls bouncing and people actually being touched by unworldly beings. Apparently, there were also sightings of Civil War soldiers and the "lady" of the hotel, but we never actually saw anything. I know that the hotel had been used during the Civil War by the Union Army for a hospital and that in 1999, during a renovation, many body parts had been discovered in the basement that had, at the time, been used as a surgical area. Body parts had been thrown under the floorboards and discovered 135 years later! There were many other examples of paranormal activity that occurred there, but the above was the extent of our experiences. It was enough for us, though. We had our fill! – *Karen H.*

## Grandma's Advice

I experienced strange things as a child that as I grew up helped form who I am. I can feel the different emotions of spirits, both dead and residual energy. This I cannot turn on or off, it happens. I found my grandmother, deceased, the day before my tenth birthday and the next day I heard her voice saying, "Baby, be good."

Hers was the first voice I heard without EVP. – *Tracy A., New York*

## Love is Forever

I lost a brother in 2000. It devastated our family, but I've watched many paranormal/ghost shows for years and I've always believed. My brother did, too. When he was a live, he would always call me in the middle of the night for my birthday. Multiple times. Lol

Several years ago, on my birthday, I decided to record a message to him. I let the recorder run a few extra minutes. When I listened to it, I was amazed and so happy with what I thought I heard. I asked if he was here with me. The voice I heard said, "Yup." Sounded just like him. I was so happy. Not telling my three kids that I even made the recording, I asked them separately to listen to it at a family BBQ. My youngest daughter was surprised. I asked her if she heard him say, "Yup," after she had listened to it.

She said, "No, Mom."

I was saddened thinking she didn't hear what I heard.

She said, "Mom. I'm hearing, 'I love you.'"

"What?"

She put my phone on speaker and turned up the volume. Sure enough. Plain as day. I heard, "I love you." Kind of in a rushed voice, but it was very clear. Made my heart so happy.

As my other two kids, at different times, came into the room, they listened. And heard the same thing. Made me so happy. – *Diane J.*

## A Creepy Campus

My name is Steve and I still to this day have never written down these experiences and have told very few people about them. Back then I didn't want folks thinking I was crazy...maybe I am. Maybe I'm not. But I know what I heard, felt, saw and experienced and it was terrifying. But now, I can't get enough experiences to end my thirst for more.

When I was nineteen years old, I was working my way through college as a nighttime campus security guard. I was a student and employee at this country's oldest military funded college, Norwich University, in Northfield, Vermont. Over its long history this campus had its share of tragedy in almost every location and building on campus. And along with the sad tales there were as many ghost stories to go along with them. At that time in my life, I was a true skeptic and still used science to explain away those things I didn't understand fully. That is until I began to work the overnight shift alone.

Many students, and others, reported strange things for almost 200 years in several of the buildings and areas. Buildings like Crawford and Partridge Halls, two connected buildings housing the now computer sciences and biology departments, the administration housing building, the Plumley Armory and the old library up on the main quad. They now have a brand-new library. The old one has become dorms. Throughout its history, the old library burned down twice, I believe, killing several people. This is where my time of becoming a true believer and now an avid amateur ghost hunter began.

It was a blisteringly cold night that December 23$^{rd}$. The temps were at about minus fifteen degrees Fahrenheit and, if you know how cold that is, you know that everything cracks and creaks, even the trees in a breeze. I was literally the only one on the campus since it was the middle of the Christmas break. Patrolling thirty-six acres alone at night can be creepy enough but I was never one to be afraid of the dark. It was about 12:15 a.m. and I was making my rounds on the upper quad. I had to enter and walk each building several times a night, checking doors and windows for any type of forced entry. At that time, we had issues with towns children messing around with things when the campus was quiet.

As I walked quietly listening and freezing, I approached the old library as always. And as always, I viewed which lights were left on in the lower floors so, of course, I went to turn them out. Now what I didn't know at that time was the lights burning, even when this building was empty, had been going on for decades. So, without a worry, I entered the library and continued downstairs where I found a restroom light on. No biggie, I thought, and turned it out, checked the floor and proceeded to leave. I left the main entrance of the old brick building and as I walked past to the left, I looked down and noticed that same light was on once again. At this time, I started to have some concern that an actual person might be in the building, so I snuck around to the back door, entered silently, and went to the restroom again. I found no one. I again turned out the light but this time I walked each floor entirely and found not a living soul.

I figured all was well and old buildings are what they are . . . well, they can be a lot more. I began to walk out of the main entrance once again but this time I heard a loud bang to the rear of the main floor. I quietly but quickly ran to the back figuring I'd catch someone messing about but there was no one.

I searched and found a large hardcover book had fallen off one of the shelves. Okay, so at this time I was getting a bit of that creepy feeling, but I picked it up, put it back and slowly began the walk out once more. As I was leaving, I heard a banging noise that was steady and loud coming from the office in the front. I figured the old steam heat pipes must be to blame but I quietly went to investigate. Behind the checkout desk are wood floors that creak a certain way when stepped on. I walked in, they creaked, and as I entered the office the banging stopped. I stood there, listening, and began to hear the distinct sound of those same floorboards creaking just like when I walked on them two minutes prior.

Well, the hair began to stand up all over my body, and I felt a freezing cold run through me. I turned to leave, scared now, and was stopped dead in my tracks. Knocking was coming from the office. I went back. No one was there and, once again, it stopped. I admit now I was creeped out and wanted to leave. As I started out of the office, I was stopped by something I couldn't believe. No air was moving. No fans were going. But as I looked up four of the big paper snowflake decorations that were hung from the ceiling were not just spinning like mad but swinging full 360s. Intentionally.

The banging began again in the front office and damned if those floorboards didn't start to creak behind the counter. I knew what was happening. Who, or whatever it was, was taunting the hell out of me. At that point I was done. I literally said, "Okay, Whoever. You can have the library tonight. I am outta here!!" and I ran to the front door, locked it, and left. But I knew at that moment there was an afterlife and ghosts are real.

However, this little story isn't over. ;) The next morning, I told my boss what happened. He wasn't surprised at all and told me he himself had many experiences over his twenty years there and many took place in that library. This helped me to believe even more strongly in the supernatural.

The next night I showed up for work at midnight, as usual. Once again all alone on campus, a super cold night and being Christmas Eve, it was as quiet as a tomb. I admit I avoided the library that night and only did outdoor and window checks, but that light was on again. My most profound experience was about to happen in a building called Partridge Hall. This was the computer science hall and one of the oldest on campus.

I was doing a motor patrol off the campus and old graveyard

when I received an automated page that the alarm was going off in one of the computer lab rooms in Partridge. I, of course, motivated myself and got there very quickly. I was very good at catching folks in the act, and I wanted to make sure this time was no different. The entire building was dark. The rooms all have heavy wood doors, and the computer rooms are the same with state-of-the-art alarm systems. This room had a heavy glass exit to the outside as well, so I was sure someone had broken in.

I approached the inside entrance to the room and could hear the alarm beeping loudly inside. I stepped inside the room, mag light in hand, and switched on the lights. No one was there. Nothing. Not even the air was moving. I turned off the alarm and checked every window and door – all tight and locked solid. These alarms don't go off for no reason, so I made damned sure everything was solid and in place. I decided it was a false notification, flipped off the lights and started resetting the alarm.

At the time I didn't really notice but all the hair on my arms, back and neck began to lift. Cold air can have that effect so, like I said, I didn't think about it. I was still pumped up from the situation. I checked once again to be sure, then locked the door behind me. Within two seconds I heard the loudest, God-awful BANG!! It literally shook the door like someone had thrown something like a basketball full force against it directly behind me. It was so startling I jumped almost six feet and hit the opposite wall.

I got myself together and threw open the door, turned on the lights, and no one was there! I said to myself, "There has to be someone," over and over as I began to kind of hyperventilate from the shock.

I know this sounds funny but whatever hit that door, or wall, hit it hard enough to knock a can of Coke from the old soda machine next to the door. I never heard it fall due the loudness of the slam, but there it was. Ice cold and waiting for me. I reset the alarm and grabbed that Coke. I said screw you and thank you for the soda and walked my ass out of that hall as quickly as I could.

There are few more minor experiences that occurred prior to my leaving that job but there is no room in this story for all of those. I have since been on over thirty-five ghost hunts and have self-hunted about 150 haunted locations around the country. I always stay in the most haunted hotels and towns in America and visit as many cool places as I can. I have, in fact, caught some great pics and sounds but it's the experiences I've had that drive me now more than ever to have more. – *Steven B., Oregon*

## A Distorted Recording

I was up in Georgia for my friend's wedding and my friend had told us stories of an abandoned church and graveyard that are close to her property. One night while we were there, three other girls and I visited this church to see if we would experience anything. The whole church felt off since we arrived, and I felt uneasy the entire time.

Upon not experiencing anything, not even on my personal spirit box, we headed back, but when I watched the videos that I had taken on my phone, my friend's voice altered in a way that sounded utterly scary and warped. This video was taken when we were first entering the church.

Not the scariest story but it's the biggest piece of evidence I had with an encounter. I've never had any auditory defects on my phone before and through my five years of having this phone it has never had the same auditory warp happen again. – *Shaylyn B., Arizona*

## Who Threw That?

I spent the night in an old house that my friend's grandma owned in Prescott, Oregon. The house was built on the site of a very old hospital. We all slept on the floor upstairs above the basement and we could hear a little girl singing.

We were home alone.

Finally, we were brave enough to investigate and we slowly walked down the stairs to the basement and turned the corner. One of the outdoor furniture cushions that was being stored flew across the room! We ran back upstairs so fast! – *Sierra A., Oregon*

# Civil War Soldier

The Bath National Cemetery, which is associated with the Bath VA Center in Bath, NY., contains soldier burials dating from the late 1700s to present day. I drive through there occasionally, paying my respects to those who served our country – at one time or another, in one capacity or another.

I visited the Bath National Cemetery one time with my younger daughter Cari and her friend Angel. They were only age twelve at the time, but I had already instilled in both of my daughters the love of visiting cemeteries. In the center of the cemetery was a hill with a road that curved around the middle of the hill and a funeral pavilion at one spot on that road. There are sections/rows of gravestones above that road and more gravestones below it. Another road went from the top straight down the right side to the bottom of the hill.

Driving down the side road that day, a spirit called out to Cari. He said his name was Cassidy. I went online to findagrave.com and found five soldiers with the last name Cassidy buried in Bath National Cemetery. Without Cari's knowledge, I wrote into my notebook the names of each Cassidy and their locations in the cemetery – section, row, stone.

Soon after my research, Cari and I went back to the Bath National Cemetery looking for the Cassidy who had reached out to her. We parked on that road at the middle of the hill near the pavilion. We had started walking up to the rows of gravestones above the road when Cari stopped abruptly. "Cassidy is not up here." Cari told me. "He is down below this road. He came to me from here because this is the only place he could project to that would reach me."

We walked back down the hill, across the road, and started down to the section of gravestones below the road. I was quietly getting excited because I knew that my notebook said one of the Cassidys was indeed buried in this section. My heart started racing knowing this information, but I kept on my poker face and walked behind Cari as she walked over to the rows of stones. She walked past some of the rows from behind and stopped at one row. "He's here," she said confidently. She started walking forward down that row.

I knew that one of the Cassidys was buried in this row. I tried hard to contain my expression. (Is an anti-expression a thing? Even more guarded than a poker face?) I silently counted about halfway down the row of stones and saw exactly where this Cassidy was buried. Cari still didn't have a clue that I knew his location. Cari walked slowly down the row of stones, then stopped. She pointed to a stone about four stones away from her. "He's buried right there." She was dead on. THAT was Michael Cassidy. And when she had first pointed out his gravestone, she had been standing to the side, far enough away that she couldn't have seen his name on the front of the stone.

CASSIDY, MICHAEL
Rank & Branch: PVT CO F 69 NY INF   US ARMY
Date of Death: 09/12/1898
Buried At: SECTION E ROW 10 SITE 15

Cari and I sat in the grass near Michael Cassidy. I couldn't hear Michael speak, but Cari could. She isn't good with asking questions of spirit, so I do that. We have used this technique in other locations, such as "Hellmira," the Civil War prisoner camp in Elmira,

New York. We make a good team in that sense!

I asked Michael why he reached out to Cari. He told Cari that she is a reincarnation of his best friend Robert. Michael further explained that he and Robert had joined the Army at the same time during the Civil War. He said Robert was the type that wanted to charge the hill first. Robert bravely charged forth into battle... but didn't make it out.

I suggested to Cari that we ask Michael if Robert was also buried in the Bath National Cemetery so we could find his grave. Cari was quite emphatic about not wanting to take that step. She felt it would be too spooky to see her own grave.

I did online research on Michael's Army company. It is amazing what you can find online! Michael and Robert were part of the 69th New York Infantry Regiment – the Irish Brigade or the Fighting Irish, as was immortalized in Joyce Kilmer's poem "When the 69th Comes Home" – from Brooklyn, New York. The Fighting Irish had a motto: Gentle When Stroked; Fierce when Provoked. The 69th even has its own whiskey!

Eventually, Cari and I went back to visit Michael Cassidy about a year later. Michael didn't reach out to Cari this time, and I couldn't coax him to join us. Cari told me that he was no longer there; he had moved on. We thought that Michael had reached out to Cari because he knew she was there and needed to tell her one of the chapters of her own reincarnation story. At age twelve, she already had reincarnation flashbacks to Ancient Egypt, the Roaring 20s in Corning, NY, being in the military and going down in a WW2 war ship, so this was added validation of yet another life. – *Tamora L. Vang, New York*

## The Impatient Guest

I threw a Halloween party and there were over thirty people in my basement. During the party we heard a scream come from upstairs. Then, all the lights blew. My fiancé got the lights turned on and we ran upstairs. The friend who had screamed told us that she was putting in her contacts when she heard someone in the kitchen making annoying sounds and attempting to open the door to the bathroom. She said she got annoyed and yelled, "Hold on! I'll be done soon!" When she opened the door, no one was there. That's when she let out a scream. She refuses to visit me. – *Maura C.*

## Room Thirteen

My dad worked a lot of overtime, fifty miles from home, so he started staying at a little place that had a few rooms to rent. Room thirteen was never rented out, but he convinced them to let him stay there. I was with him one night and he told me about odd things that happened. While I was there, the toilet flushed by itself and the metal hangers in the closet started banging together, even though the door was closed. – *Kim S., Michigan*

## Did You Hear It?

My mother died. The next morning at her house, my daughter and I were getting ready to go back to the hospital. My granddaughter had taken ill, too, and we were getting things ready for the hospital. I was drinking coffee in the kitchen. My daughter was in the bedroom and, plain as day, my mother's voice called out my name with my middle name, too, clear as anything. My daughter came from the bedroom and looked around the doorway. I was standing there, frozen.

I looked at her and asked, "Did you hear it?"

She said, "Yes, as plain as we are talking." – *Jonnie S.*

## Patrolling the Bay

I used to work as an EMT and the station I worked at was haunted. We would hear footsteps walking down the hall and no one would be there. Our garage door would raise up by itself and we would think we had an emergency call and go out to the bay and neither one of us had raised the door.

One time, I heard the front door open and footsteps coming down the hall. They stopped at my door, so I opened the door really fast. No one was there. Another time I heard scratching on my window, and I went outside to investigate. No one was there.

No one wanted to stay there at night. It was a creepy place. – *Karen S., Oklahoma*

## The Haunting of Shore House

My wife, Jennifer, is from the Downeast coast of Maine. Before coming up here four years ago to care for her parents, we spent most of each summer at her birthplace. It was during one of these visits, we had the chance to investigate an historic house on the coast. The house had been owned by the sister of a very famous American doctor and writer whose name was common, spoken and read. I do not want to say more because the house is currently owned by another family who knows nothing of this tale. When the good doctor's sister passed away, she left the home to a friend of ours, Kim Smith, who was her caregiver. Kim had many previous experiences in the house with unexplained noises and was excited to see what we could discover. She was getting the house ready to sell and agreed to an investigation, and willingly participated.

The first time we investigated the house and grounds, nothing happened. Well, not much happened. I didn't catch any EVPs, pictures or video evidence other than a few orbs. But we all shared a feeling of an electric charge in the air upstairs. When you enter the huge living room, you have two options to go upstairs. You can enter via a stairway or go upstairs to a landing where you will find two bedrooms and a full bath. You can exit the way you came or exit the other set of stairs. Yes, all the stairs creaked. It was while standing on this hallway landing that all of us experienced a feeling that we were not alone. We all experienced goosebumps and the hair on our necks and arms was standing straight up. The air wasn't heavy or foreboding but simply charged with electricity. We discussed the feeling in depth but received no evidence to validate our feelings.

Fast forward a year. We knew that Kim had a buyer lined up for the house and we wanted one more shot at investigating this home. I was thoroughly surprised the first time that we were unable to document any paranormal activity and I wanted a do-over. This house had stood too long not to have some kind of energy inside. We all agreed to meet one more time and see what we might be lucky enough to find.

The investigation went much like the first one. The energy upstairs was off the chart. Each of us had the same, if not more powerful, reactions to being on the landing as the last time. Goosebumps, hair standing straight and convinced in our minds that someone was about to step out from around a corner anytime. I received no visual evidence. No video nor photographic evidence was captured. The audio evidence would have to wait for the next day as that part is a time-consuming process. We left the landing and relocated to the living room where the conversation about the energy in the house continued. I left the recorder going during this conversation. That decision paid off well.

The next day, I set aside time to review the audio recordings. It can take hours to review minutes of audio. I always attempt to get everyone to speak in their normal voice during investigations because it makes it easier to pick the subtle sounds out. You do not always get a clear EVP. During the review, I listen with headphones on and the volume all the way up.

I was sitting at my writing desk, playing, rewinding, and

playing again until I got to the conversation we had in the living room. It was while listening to this portion of the recording that I did something I have never done before. I jerked the headphones off, threw them down and ran. Yep, that describes it perfectly. That feeling we had on the landing returned. Every hair on my body was standing up and I was covered with goosebumps. With mouth agape, I stared at the headphones like they were going to attack me.

It took a good fifteen minutes before I gathered the gumption to listen to the EVP once again. It was still there, and it was unbelievable. You can hear Jennifer and Kim talking to each other about the feelings we experienced upstairs, when a new female voice talks over the top of them and says, "The door...there is someone at the door upstairs." It was so clear that it sounded like she was standing beside us, and I guess she was. To be honest, I still get goosebumps as I type the tale. – *Richard D. Rowland, author of Unspoken Messages: Spiritual Lessons I Learned from Horses and Other Earthbound Souls. You can listen to the EVP at* https://richarddrowlandbooks.com/the-haunting-of-shore-house/ .

## A Baby's Cry

When I was in grade school we lived in a house where every night at 2:00 a.m. a baby would cry and wake all of us up. I was the youngest in the house and I was eight years old. We lived there for about five years, and it happened every night. We never found where the sound came from. You could be in the living room and the sound would be in the bedroom. You could go to the bedroom and the sound would then come from the kitchen. The people that moved into the house after us only lived there for a month. My dad always said it wasn't there to cause us harm. – *Henry R.*

## No One There

When I was a teenager, I used to hang out at my cousin's house quite a bit, as did many of our mutual friends. We had heard stories of the house being haunted but didn't think much about it. One evening, a friend and I went over there to hang out, but my cousin wasn't home yet, so my aunt said we could hang out until she got home.

We were sitting in her room talking and whatnot while we were waiting for her to get home. Out of the blue, we heard a knock on the other side of the wall. At first, we thought it was her brother messing with us. He hadn't been home when we got there...it was just us and her mom, who was downstairs. But we thought maybe he came home and snuck up the stairs since we didn't hear anyone walk up them (they were creaky, metal stairs and he was a big guy so it was pretty unlikely that he could pull that off).

We started taking turns knocking back and forth with whoever was on the other side of the wall. I finally decided to get up and told my friend to knock on the wall again, that I would open the door really quickly and scare whoever it was. When I opened the door, however, no one was there...and there was absolutely no way anyone would have had enough time to run off or hide as it is an open area at the top of the stairs.

We also used to see shadows moving around in the corner of the ceiling at night when the lights were off and we were trying to go to sleep, so there is no doubt in my mind that the house was indeed haunted. – *Rebecca J., Iowa*

## Last One Turns Out the Lights

I believe that the events that happened in my house between 2008-2016 were by my mom based on the items involved. I'll list them...

A big plastic ashtray my mom swiped from a pub in England (where she was from and had been visiting family at the time) that she had given to me, flew across the room one morning. At the time, I was online and making a big deal to friends about a certain song that was popular on my birthday (I had thought it was another) and mentioned my mom in regard to it. As I walked into the kitchen, I heard something crash in the living room. When I looked, the ashtray that had been sitting on a bookshelf, was now across the room twenty feet away, laying on the floor!

On my fiftieth birthday, I woke up a little depressed. When I went into the living room, I sat down on the couch and happened to look up to see the big antique Maxfield Parrish print my mom had given to me for my birthday about fifteen years previous, hanging cockeyed! It had been hanging straight the night before. Mom was probably wishing me a happy one.

I was having an emotional day in regard to my mom when a neighbor (who was a single mother with a few kids) was having a rough day with her kids and I could hear her yelling at them. It got me thinking about my mom and how I was such a sh*t as a teenager and put her through a lot. I was standing in my kitchen and said aloud how sorry I was for what I put her through. Then, a moment later, I heard three knocks on my living room wall. They were "sloppy" knocks as if someone was hitting up against the wall with a limp backhand. I felt that was my mom letting me know she heard me.

My stepdad passed away about ten years after my mom did. Six months later, I was reading in my bed as I usually do before I go to sleep. About twenty minutes in, the light went off. This was a "touch" lamp. At first, I thought the power went off, but I saw my clock radio was on! Earlier that day I had been watching an episode of "Celebrity Ghost Stories" and it featured Rue McClanahan who talked about a friend of hers who told her and his other friends that after he died, he would try to reach them through electricity. I was pretty amazed by how he reached out to her and the others with what he did. Then, I got my own "electric" encounter. That touch lamp had never done that before or in the last five years since. I haven't had anymore (noticed) experiences since then. Maybe it was my mom and (now) stepdad letting me know… "last one out turns out the lights." — *Mickey W., Texas*

## The Ghost at Maggie's Bridge

My friends and I decided to head over to Delaware to investigate what they call Maggie's Bridge. Her ghost is said to haunt the bridge in search of her baby. As the legend goes, you're supposed to say, "Maggie, I have your baby," and she will appear. We did just that and, as the night grew darker, things got bizarre.

First, using my friend's spirit box, we heard a woman speaking through it. We kept trying to get the conversation going but it eventually stopped. We also kept hearing weird noises coming from the woods. Next came the craziest experience I've had, and we caught it on camera.

I set up my night vision camera on the hood of my friend's truck. I also had my charger plugged in and made sure it was stable. As we walked away and did another session, we heard a loud bang come from the truck area. We went back to see what happened and my camera and charger were on the ground. Luckily my friend had his dashcam rolling and, when we checked the footage, it appeared that the camera and charger were thrown off his truck…and at a decent distance, too. We double checked to make sure it didn't just fall off but there was no way. It had been stable. I'll never forget that investigation. — *Chris B., New Jersey*

## Dad's Cigarettes and Mom's Hello

I'm from Monroe in Orange County, New York. I grew up

on a dirt road in the woods. From a young age I have seen shadow people, heard noises and seen things I couldn't explain. I have come to learn that I am an empath medium.

In the early 1990s, my uncle passed and following his passing, I would see shadow people hiding behind trees on my property. When my dad passed in our home about eleven years ago, I smelled his cigarettes for a very long time. He quit smoking before he got sick, so it had been quite a long time since there was that smell in the house.

Years later, my mother passed and one day I was in my car, parked, and I had the radio on. I very clearly heard my mother come through the radio and say my name. It scared me so badly I started to cry. – *Dolores F., New York*

## The Man of the House Hasn't Gone

I moved into the lower level of a duplex in October of 2000 with my cat, Maxwell. The landlady told me the husband of the prior tenant had passed away and the woman and her two children moved. I was there about two weeks before anything happened.

My apartment was a two bedroom. When you went down the stairs, the living room and kitchen were to the left and the two beds and bath were down a short hall to the right. The bath had a doorway to the hall and one to the master bedroom. I had a nightlight in the bathroom, so I kept the door shut so the light did not shine into my room.

One night, the door from the master to the bath flew open and banged, hard, into the tub. Hard enough to make a mark on the door. I opened my eyes to see nothing but my cat, fur puffed up, growling. I could see into the bathroom. There was nothing. I could see the light in the hall and waited for a shadow. Nothing. After a few minutes, I got up the nerve to go look. Still nothing. No one there. The windows were all closed so there was no breeze.

It scared the hell out of me.

Only a couple of nights later, I woke up to the sound of my toilet flushing. Again, I stared at the light in the hall and saw nothing. I went to look and the toilet seats were up, like when a man uses the toilet. Neither I, nor my cat, ever did that.

All was quiet for a week.

One night, when I was asleep, I heard a loud boom next to my bed. I mean right next to my bed. Sweating and shaking, I reached across that small gap between the bed and nightstand to turn on the light. Again, nothing was there or out of place on the floor. – *Judy D.*

## The Call Button

Many years ago, I was working in a long-term care facility on second shift. My coworker and I had finished our rounds and we were standing at the nurses' station when we heard a call light go off. We looked down the hall and saw what room the light was coming from and stared at each other. The day before, a lady had passed away in that room and it was empty. She did not have a roommate. We went down the hall, looked into the room and didn't see anyone. The call lights were the old ones that had to be pushed in to work. We turned it off and left the room, thinking it was weird.

When we got back down to the nurses' station, it went off again. We checked it out and it was the same thing...no one was there. We headed back, looked at each other, and said, "If that goes off again, we're unplugging the light from the wall." Sure enough, not five minutes later, it happened once more.

We walked to the room. I went in and turned off the call light. My coworker stood outside of the room. I unplugged the call light from the wall. A call light dinged.

I said, "Tell me it's not coming from this room."

She looked at me. "Yes, it is."

The call light was going and we couldn't shut it off so, at this point, I started talking. I said the lady's name (which I do not remember now) and told her, "It's okay to go be with your family, and all of the people you have lost, in heaven. Go be at peace." The light shut off and never turned back on by itself. – *Sue W., Missouri*

## I've Got It, Dad

I had some [experiences]. Never got scared of it happening. I was gone for a long time from my parents' home and came back to take care of my mom. Early one morning I poured a cup of coffee in my dad's cup. As I turned away, I watched the cup slide across the table. Then saw my dad's chair scoot up by itself. The cup spun around to face the empty chair. So, I calmly grabbed another cup and filled it, then went to the cup that slid across the table. I took a spoonful out, threw it into the woodstove and said, "Thank you, Dad. I am home to take care of Mom now. You've got nothing to worry about. Everything will be okay now. No one will hurt my mom again ever."

After doing that, I never saw anything move around but always heard footsteps walking by my room and then leaving again. – *Alphonse E.*

## A Whistling Ghost

As a young woman, around seventeen or eighteen years old, I rented a house in Arkansas. I was in the home one day, took a nap and woke to whistling (thought it was a bird). I listened harder and it seemed more like a person whistling a tune. It stopped and I heard what sounded like heavy boots walking in the house on my linoleum floors. I checked doors, windows, and locks and didn't see anything. Days later, my roommate said they were told by someone who previously lived there that it was haunted. I said, "April fools. Right."

I said if they left me alone, I'd do the same. It was the day before April 1st.

The next morning, I was woken up to the house being on fire. My roommate had fallen asleep with a cigarette. I never saw anyone around outside the house when I heard the footsteps or whistling. – *Angela C., Kansas*

## Some New Orleans Magic

My husband and I bought our current home during the Spring of 2016. We lived here uneventfully until the Summer of 2019. During that summer break, my husband and I went to the beach (Gulf Shores, Alabama) with our family and then, later in July, I went with some friends to New Orleans for a week. While in New Orleans, we stayed in an older hotel off Canal Street and took in the sights every day. One of the girls on the trip was quite eccentric and wanted to visit cemeteries, Voodoo shops, etc. We kept putting her off until, finally, we caved and went on a ghost tour. The tour was uneventful, but we ended up having a good time. It was more of a history lesson than anything else.

After I returned home from New Orleans, I was off for a few weeks and then I went back to work as a teacher before the beginning of the school year. My husband and I got back into the routine of getting up at 6:00 a.m. and things were fine until I had the Friday off before the semester started. We discussed over dinner, outside of the home, that we were going to sleep in the next day.

The next morning, an alarm went off at 6:00 a.m., and we couldn't figure out where it was coming from. We got up, started going from room to room, and finally my husband found the source. It was an old alarm clock that I kept on the vanity in the bathroom. My husband asked if I had set it, but I was as dumbfounded as he was. The clock was at least thirty years old, and I received it as a gift from my grandparents. I didn't use it as an alarm, but it was pretty, so

I kept it on the vanity as a timepiece and for decoration. We struggled to figure out how to turn it off since it had been so long since we had used it. I accused my kids of setting it. Both were just as confused as we were. I assumed we would never know why it went off.

A few weeks later, we were back in the school routine, and I was having trouble sleeping. I got up about 3:30 a.m., took some Tylenol and laid back down. I apparently had not set my alarm the night before and neither had my husband. I was actually getting the best sleep I'd had in a while when there was a sharp knock on the headboard right above my head. I jerked awake and looked over to see my husband facing the opposite direction. I asked him why he knocked on the headboard. He rolled over and said he hadn't. I was laying there furious with him for waking me up before the alarm went off, and when I looked to see what time it was, I realized that we overslept. I started yelling for him to get up, that we were late and, on the way to work in the car, I asked, "Are you sure you didn't knock on the headboard?" He swore he didn't.

After that, things happened regularly around the house...too numerous to list but some of the things that stand out were my husband's keys being lifted off the wall hanger and left in the middle of the floor, fifteen feet away, doors opening and closing on their own, I was touched one evening on my rear end while cooking supper (being the only one at home), and lots of noises that we couldn't account for.

Every time I had an encounter or event, I would tell my friends at work. One of them had a friend who was a paranormal investigator from central Arkansas. She asked if I minded if she told her my story, which I said was fine. A few days later, Nancy asked if I would be willing to call her friend and tell her my stories firsthand. I said sure. I called later that evening and we talked at length about my problem. She said that she was also a medium and while talking to me she was picking up that this guy had attached himself to me when I was out somewhere. She asked when this all started, and I said after my trip to New Orleans. She told me that totally made sense, but I could have picked him up somewhere else. She couldn't be sure. She asked if I liked to shop at auctions or estate sales. I told her no, but I do shop at thrift stores for furniture or antiques. She basically said that he encountered me somewhere and that he really liked me and wanted to help me by waking me up so I wouldn't be late, but why the other things were going on could be his way of letting me know he's still around. She didn't feel the need to come investigate as long as I wasn't scared or anything. So, we left it at that.

A few weeks later, I was putting up my Christmas tree and afterwards my friend called from Arizona. I was sitting on the couch, talking, admiring the tree. The subject of my ghost came up. She asked if he had done anything lately? I said no and that I thought I might have run him off. She responded, "Good." I told her that it made me kind of sad. She asked why, and I basically said that I didn't mind him being around and if being here made him comfortable, I was okay with that. I really wished I knew who he was when he was alive and where I had picked him up. Her response was that I might not ever know.

Whenever I travel, I purchase a Christmas ornament to mark the occasion. The New Orleans trip was no different. So that afternoon, after the conversation with my friend, my younger daughter and I went shopping, picked up some gifts and attended a birthday party. No one was home the entire time we were out. When we returned, she went to her room, and I started cooking supper. I stepped into the dining room, which is near the living room, and as I turned around, I saw the New Orleans Christmas ornament (that I had hanging a good two inches deep on the branch near the top of the tree) on the floor nearly ten feet away from the tree. You couldn't miss it! We do have a dog, but she is small. The ornament was hanging at my eye level, which is 5'5" on a seven-foot tree, and it was the ONLY ornament that was "knocked" off the tree. In fact, I'm not sure a child could have moved the ornament. I felt that "He" heard my conversation and knew that he could at least let me know where I had encountered him.

Things have slowed down significantly over the past few months. I'm not sure if he is even still with us. Every now and then I'll hear something in another part of the house, or I'll catch the dog looking at something across the room. I may never know who he was when he was alive but as far as I'm concerned, he was a great experience and wasn't scary at all. – *Jodi D., Arkansas*

## A Hello from Mom

I was taking a nap after work last week. I was laying on our couch when I heard my name called.

"Michael!"

It woke me up. I thought my wife had gotten home from work but that wasn't the case. It was loud enough to wake me up out of sleep. We have some items from my mom in our apartment from when she passed away years ago…her glasses, her high school graduation photo and a couple of other items. I believe she came to visit me. This wasn't the first instance. – *Michael P.*

## Who's Calling?

About two years ago I moved in with my daughter and her family. It was my second night in my bedroom there and I woke up hearing this loud, but softly spoken, woman calling me. She said, "Deborah…where are you?" It had an echo to it and sounded ghostly. I heard it about three times and swear I heard it as I was waking up. I turned over to see who was there. There was no one and the voice stopped.

I was tired from moving and I didn't care whether there was a ghost there or not. I just went back to sleep. The next day I told my oldest granddaughter and she said she always heard her name being called when she used to sleep in that room. Maybe I wasn't dreaming. Maybe it was real! – *Deborah F., Idaho*

# Stay Out of My Room

My then fiancée and I moved above the Golden Lion Lounge in the spring of 2010. He was to run daily operations and bartend. The apartment came rent-free as part of his payment, and the obvious close location made it convenient. It was an amazing deal for us. I was between serving jobs at the time, and we were planning and saving for a wedding. We recruited some family and a close friend of ours to help with the move.

I had only been in the main room, the one that you enter from the main door, once. So, I never had a chance to fully explore before moving in, which, looking back, I guess is kinda odd. We had an outdoor entrance that led up a flight of stairs and to a breezeway, which led to our front entrance. Both doors locked. The layout of the place was a circle, all doors continuously leading to the next room, except the kitchen and bathroom.

After we had moved all our boxes in, our friend and I decided to explore, since I hadn't yet had the chance. We were like little kids running through the place. We ran into a large room off what became our TV room and that's when we noticed another door leading off that room. The door was open. We, including my dog, went to the doorway. All three of us stopped dead in our tracks at the threshold, as if something, or some force, stopped us from entering. We looked at each other thinking, "Did you feel that as well??"

We leaned in and looked. It was a smaller, closet-style room. The door at the other end led into what would become our bedroom. But something felt off. Call it intuition. We decided we would never use that room. I shut the door, never to open it again. We used the room it was off for storage, and I ended up putting a dresser in front of the entrance from our bedroom.

Now, whenever I had to put something in that main storage room, I moved fast! I always had the odd feeling that something in the shadows was watching me. When I went to bed at night, I would stare at the door behind the dresser, waiting for something to jump out and kill me. Granted, I've had an overactive imagination since I was a youngster. When we would be in our TV room, our Lab would lay on the floor, staring at the storage room door as if guarding us, while also keeping himself at a safe distance. He would occasionally bark or gruff at the door, clearly upset by something, while also solidifying my idea that something was off. I would swear I could hear noises, footsteps, etc. I was told, "Maybe animals?" or, "We live above a bar. I don't hear anything weird." I would see things in my peripheral vision in the little window above the door. I'd turn to look and there'd be nothing there. But my dog continued to stand guard.

Then, finally, our day came! 10-10-10, our wedding day! It went great, seamless and magical. As it should be. We came home that Sunday, after our obligatory stay in a hotel. Reveling in our joy, we checked out all our wedding gifts and opened our cards. We finally got hungry and headed off to a late-night diner. After we enjoyed our 2:00 a.m. greasy breakfast, we headed home. We went to the outside entrance, up to the breezeway and opened our front door.

To our bewilderment EVERY cabinet door, drawer, medicine cabinet, dresser drawer, entertainment drawer, etc., was wide open. In every room. Our entrances had been locked. We knew that. It was a top floor with no way to break in. The only window that would work, you'd have to be Spiderman to enter. Scale a wall while opening a window and pushing out an air conditioner with one hand to even enter the building. Then, somehow leave and lock deadbolts? The wedding presents were laying unscathed on the floor below that window. Nothing was stolen. All money and presents were accounted for. And I received a Cadillac blue Kitchen Aid mixer. You'd have to be nuts not to steal that.

We noticed all the doors were closed. Bathroom door, bedroom door. All except the door to the closet room. That was wide open. We freaked out! We grabbed our dogs and ran out to our car. We called our friend, the one who helped us move. He was the "not too scared of anything" type. He was over in fifteen minutes, carrying a katana sword. Naturally. He explored every room. No robber, no sign of a break in. We went back up, closed all our cabinets and drawers and we cracked open a beer to try to calm down. We had an old-fashioned slumber party. Power in numbers.

Two months later, we moved out. The owner had decided to shut the bar down. I was glad to be gone. I still heard footsteps, noises, etc. My dog would still stand guard and occasionally bark. I figured, well, something doesn't like us here.

I began asking people who had lived there before about it. Prior managers and helpers. One friend said he had no problems at all. He used my "hell room" as an exercise room. I asked an old manager about his experiences. He replied, "Are you asking if it's haunted? I don't know about that. But I'll tell you, I did everything not to sleep there." Another friend told me he would sometimes wake up and feel as if something was on his chest. He had trouble breathing. He would pray or ask it to stop, and it would. But he would also get mysterious scratches and swore up and down he saw words trying to manifest on the bathroom mirror after a shower.

The Lions was bought and renovated. The new owner told me to come in and see what he had done to the place. It was beautiful! Completely different. However, he did have an interesting tale to tell. When they lifted the floor of the old office, they found an unmarked gravestone. NO body. Just the stone. I asked him if he was serious. He laughed. To this day I don't know if he was telling the truth, but every time I pass the building and look up, I expect something, or someone, to be staring back at me from that window.
— *Allyson W., Ohio*


# A Violent End

I moved into a new home in 1987. It was a sunny day, and the house was everything my children and I needed. The prior owner mentioned to us that he had lost a son to suicide. He didn't tell us where it happened but by the time I moved out twenty-three years later, I knew. I have had paranormal experiences all my life but surprisingly did not pick up on anything that day. Looking back on it all I should have asked for more details, but it was a difficult subject for the gentleman and the house was lovely.

Many of the experiences in the house occurred with my animals around, with them alerting me or going through it with me. One night, I was lying on the couch watching TV while my cat was sitting on top of it. She appeared to be watching something. I glanced up. A large black mass was moving across the ceiling and went through the wall.

On another occasion, my dog and I were sitting on the couch late at night when I heard the kitchen door open and a deep, male, booming voice said, "Hey!" It startled both myself and my dog. We looked at each other in shock. Normally she was a great watchdog, but she was absolutely terrified, as was I. Her hair stood up; her eyes were wide. She was shaking. I thought an intruder had broken in. Reluctantly I got up to face whoever was in the kitchen, but the dog wouldn't budge. She dug her feet into the carpet as I tried to take her with me. She wouldn't have been much help, but I was scared to go out there alone. I dragged her with me, and I do mean dragged.

We got to the kitchen and there was nothing. Absolutely nothing. That voice had been loud, clear and aggressive.

Over the years, the kids and I switched bedrooms. I was sleeping in the master bedroom one night when around 3:00 a.m. I woke to feel someone or something sitting at the foot of my bed. I felt the bed pressed down at my feet. This was the only time that I could not look. I thought if I saw someone sitting there, I would die of a heart attack. I went under the covers and stayed there for quite some time.

The following I find to be the most profound of my experiences. I moved to the upstairs bedroom where the sons of the prior owner had slept. When we moved in, the carpet had been removed and the wall board taken off, exposing the bare wood. Only later did I think to myself, "Death scene cleanup?" I didn't think a lot about it in the beginning.

Once I started sleeping in this room, I had nightly experiences. I would turn out the light and get comfortable, then in the corner were clicking sounds, sparks and flashes. Gun! Once my body started to relax for sleep, something would slap my pillow above my head and continue all around my body, head to foot. After that happened, it would quiet down and, eventually, I would go to sleep. This happened nightly.

Sounds like a residual haunt, doesn't it? Well, it didn't feel that way to me. One night the slap above my head was particularly hard. I turned on the light and shouted, "I heard that!" I began to feel as if I was sleeping in someone else's room and maybe he didn't like it.

The nightly routine continued, and I finally called the City Genealogical Society to see what I could find out. I could not get death certificates as they are not available for seventy-five years, but I did get names, birth dates and death dates. The newest date of death was a son who died in the same year we moved in. 1987. His birthday was two months before mine. The suicide was the only death in the house that seemed recent.

I began to wonder if this was happening to me because I was near his age, or did he resent me for sleeping in his room? My children had previously slept in that room and had experiences different from mine. I always wished that I knew the why of it all. I believe with all my heart that the son shot himself in the corner of that room. All activity took place in that corner... the click, the flash and the sparks. I have a lot of compassion for the boy. Of course, he came home to his room after the trauma of such a death...and we unknowingly moved right into his house and bedroom. I believe he was reliving his traumatic death nightly and was not at rest. How terribly sad!

My children and I experienced other things, such as pounding footsteps on the basement floor, my cat growling in that particular bedroom corner each night, rhythmic knocking. Two of my children saw apparitions. Objects were moved. I felt something lurking behind me and it tugged on my clothes. My son watched a spoon on the table vibrate and spin rapidly. There were many more experiences over the last twenty-three years but of all, I still think of the spirit who could not rest. I was afraid of him, which is why I only interacted with him once. I didn't want him angry. I felt pity for him, but it was a great weight off my shoulders when I moved out of the house in 2010. – *Vicki K., New York*

# 3

# DID YOU FEEL THAT?

Have you ever passed through a cold spot? An area so much chillier than the surrounding air that it made you take notice, look behind you, shudder and walk on? Have you ever been tapped on the shoulder, turned and no one was there? Or walked down rickety basement stairs, wiping cobwebs from your arms and face, only to switch on the lights…with no cobwebs or dust to be found? Have you settled in for the night only to feel someone sit on the edge of your bed, see the depression in the mattress itself, but you're alone? It may be a deceased loved one, desiring to be close, wanting to watch over you and not to disturb. Or, could it be something more sinister?

In early 1997, after a long night awake with my infant and toddler, I finally had the two asleep and settled into bed myself. My husband was sleeping in the other room, so he'd be fresh for work the next day. I rolled onto my side, checked the clock and sighed. 5:30 a.m.

Before I could shut my eyes, I felt arms wrap around me from behind, one sliding between my body and the bed, the other coming over me. A hug. The hands intertwined with mine. I was used to odd things happening in the house, but I'd never had any ghostly interaction like this before. My first thought was that it was my grandmother, since she'd been particularly active over the years, intending to comfort me after such a trying night. But when I felt breath beside my ear, my eyes went wide. It wasn't my grandmother; it was a man. I panicked and tried to yell for my husband, but no sound escaped. I was terrified.

As quickly as it was there, it was gone. 5:35 a.m. I stared at the clock, wide awake. Heart pounding. To this day, I have no idea who or what it might have been, or what its intentions were, but it hasn't happened again.

Brushes with something "felt" aren't limited to a touch from a spirit, however. In March of 2015, my husband bought a large knife at a gun and knife show. He was proud of his purchase and, when he got home, brought it out to show me. As he unsheathed it, I got a very creepy feeling...as if something was *wrong*. This was the first time I'd gotten that sense from an object. When I held it in my hand, I had to quickly put it down and wipe my hand off, down the leg of my pants. The knife felt *off*. My husband slid it down my arm and I wanted to jump out of my skin. He thought it was funny. I wanted it gone. Or cleansed. Or both. He put it away and refused to tell me where, saying he didn't want it cleansed.

Over the next two months I would wake up in the middle of the night. When I looked out into the living room and kitchen from my bed, I thought I caught sight of an "extra" shadow. Something that didn't quite belong but wasn't enough to grab my full attention. Here and there, it seemed to be getting closer to the bedroom, but I chalked it up to my being half asleep.

One day, my husband texted from work that he had a weird experience at 3:30 a.m. He had gotten up to go to the bathroom and realized that the hallway down to our children's rooms was darker than it should have been.

"Almost like the total blackness extended beyond the hallway...."

After he went to the bathroom, he returned to the living room to stare into the darkness and be certain what he was looking at wasn't some kind of optical illusion. He'd never been one to take things at face value. There was light in the living room, but it was somehow missing down the hallway. He described it as a "light-absorbing dark."

One night soon after that, I woke at 2:00 a.m. and tried to see into the living room. My entire bedroom doorway was dark. Blacker than black. Usually, you could see easily into the living room. There was always a glow from the digital clocks, the microwave. But there was nothing. I must've dozed off because at 4:30 a.m., when I looked again, everything was back to normal. Something was in my house.

My friend and fellow investigator, Tressa, said that I needed to find the knife and to sage and salt it, and to sage the house as soon as possible. I told my husband it had to be done, that something was very wrong. He reluctantly gave in. He told me where to find the knife… and admitted to hiding it under my side of the bed to see if it would give me nightmares.

After I cleansed the knife and saged, everything seemed to go back to normal. I was no longer seeing shadows in the house and the negative feeling was gone. However, for quite a while afterward when I would go outside, I sensed something was just out of sight, past the cars and toward the tree line. Watching.

Had the figure outside been attached to the knife or from somewhere else? Objects can carry negative energy, an imprint of energies that had been around them, or even have a spirit or entity attached to them. An interesting event transpired in April of 2016 when my original ghost hunting team and I were visiting Gettysburg, Pennsylvania, on a long weekend.

We had walked through the battlefield, the Wheat Field, the memorials, taken a ghost tour or two and happened upon a haunted tour of the old orphanage. We stopped in the gift shop beside the orphanage to buy our tickets for the tour later that evening. Up on a shelf were various knickknacks and I bought a little black die that had skulls for the dots. It was cute, and I thought it'd look great on a shelf at home. We took our tour and finished up our stay in Pennsylvania.

When I returned home and unpacked my things, the first

thought I had on taking the die out of my bag was, "I don't like that." That struck me as strange. Why wouldn't I like it now? I bought it for myself. Setting it to the side, I continued unpacking the rest of my bags. When it was the last thing left, I had the same feeling. "I don't like that." So, I put it on a side table and went on with my evening.

Later, when I bent over the table to plug in my phone, I sensed something. There was definitely something not right with that die. Before I went to bed, I put it on top of my bookshelf, beside a Buddha statue, a selenite tower and a protection jar (that absorbs negativity). I hoped that in the morning it would feel better. I laid in bed that night thinking that in the morning, if it hadn't eased up, I would throw it in the garbage. It only cost a few dollars. BUT what blasted across my mind was that I couldn't do that...it would be wrong. Bad. I knew I shouldn't do it. The ONLY thing that came to mind that seemed right was to send it back "where it belonged." That was it. That was what I needed to do.

When I got up in the morning, the die still felt wrong. I packed it up, saged the house, saged the box I packed it in, saged my car. I drove it straight to the post office and mailed it back to the shop where I had purchased it...with a note and no return address.

What I hadn't realized at the time was that the little shop where I bought the die had been a part of the original orphanage many years ago. I'm wondering if one of the child spirits still residing there had liked the die and came with it when I brought it home...and that was why it needed to go back "where it belonged."

As I've mentioned, ghosts, spirits, entities and energies have ways of being noticed. The following incident expanded my view and understanding of the paranormal and made me question our roles in this reality.

October 2009. I was a member of our school district's Board of Education, and we'd often have meetings that ran late into the night. After one of these meetings, I was driving along a dark, remote road to get home. Suddenly, it felt as if I had passengers in the back seat. It was as if they'd jumped into the car out of nowhere. I didn't want to look at my rearview mirror as I was sure they'd be staring back at me. I was uncomfortable but tried to shake it off as an overactive imagination and was happily relieved when I pulled into my driveway and the feeling was gone.

I didn't think about this "encounter" again until I was driving home from another late meeting and reached that same stretch of road. I had passengers again. This time, though, they were "stronger." I could tell there were three separate energies. Two were smaller, more subdued and seemed feminine, and the one sitting directly behind me I sensed as male. He was taller and more obvious than the girls. I didn't know why they were there and didn't want them going home with me, so I told them they had to leave. That they needed to get out…which they did. I drove the rest of the way home secure in the notion that I was "in control" of the situation.

I wasn't.

Nearly every time I drove by, they'd be there. I'd reach a particular spot on my drive, and I wouldn't be alone. I was talking with my niece and husband about it one Saturday night as we sat having drinks and a fire on our deck. My husband had an "eureka" moment and said, "You know, it's probably those kids who were killed in that car accident. Years ago. Where do you feel them?"

It was an oh-my-God moment, and a chill went down my spine.

My niece said, "Yeah, it is!" She is very sensitive and said she heard a collective "YES!" around her when he mentioned the accident. Like a "they got it!" exclamation.

There had been a tragic accident on that road five years earlier and three teenagers had been killed. I never connected the two events until that moment. I looked up the information on the crash. Two girls and one boy had died, as I had felt on every pass. But why were they riding with me?

The visits didn't end with the discovery. One October afternoon, I was driving two of my children home from school. Not only did I feel the one, strongest, energy jump into the car, he plowed through me. I was hit in the chest and, for a fraction of a second, it felt as if there was another set of eyes seeing through mine, before he pulled backward to sit in the seat behind me.

He definitely had my attention now.

My husband suggested we drive to the accident site and then continue on out to the lake, to "finish" the drive the kids had started five years before. It was a beautiful day and we spoke to them as we drove...getting as close to the lake as we could with the car. I'm not sure if this is what they were looking for, or if they just needed to be acknowledged, but I haven't sensed the boy or the girls since.

## A Father's Approval

Before my husband and I got married, his father passed away. We were on his couch, cuddling, when I felt someone pat me on the head. I asked my husband if he did it and he said no, but that when his father liked someone, he would pat them on the head. – *Edna W., New York*

## They Told Me They Drowned

I can see and talk to spirits, and I have since I was a little kid. One time, I went to a place with my mom, and I was drawn to the pond out back. My mom caught me staring into this pond and asked what was wrong. I told her that a little girl and boy had drowned there. She went to the owners and told them what I had said. They confirmed that a few years before there had been a flood at that location, and it took a little boy and girl with it. Since then, things like that have happened to me. – *Morgan D., West Virginia*

## Play it Again, Classically

In the late 1990s, my girlfriend and I were caretakers of a fine arts colony in Eureka Springs, Arkansas. Late in summer, after all the students and staff were gone, my girlfriend Kymbo went off onto the campus. I heard classical piano music and followed it to the basement of the girls' dorm…where I found Kymbo playing an upright in one of the rehearsal rooms.

As I leaned on the back of the piano, she started playing rock & roll. The room became so cold that we could see our breath and were chilled to the bone. We stepped outside through a basement door to a normal 75-degree afternoon. By the way, the dorm had no heat or air systems at that time.

Also, the "Den Mother" that had looked after the girls' dorm had an apartment on the first floor. I was told she died there…and is said to have been a classical/church musician. – *Victor B.*

## The Two Henrys

I have belonged to a couple of paranormal teams. The director of the team I was on at the time and I were best friends, and went out to a graveyard near our homes a few times. It's a beautiful place. Stunning at night. High on a hill behind a church in the Tennessee countryside, millions of stars illuminate the sky.

We took our equipment and headed out around 10:00 p.m. We'd been recording for a bit, hoping to catch a glimpse of something or a sound that couldn't be explained away. As we were talking and heading toward the front of the cemetery to take a quick break, I heard something. What it sounded like to me was footsteps coming up at an angle on my left side. And, since it was only the two of us, I immediately thought it was a rabbit. Remember, we're in the country.

I stopped and started panning the ground with my flashlight

to find this animal. My friend asked what was wrong and I told her. She heard nothing. As we headed off, I caught it again, only closer.

I stopped. It stopped. I asked my friend if she heard it. Again, no. This continued a few more times. Each time, the rustling came more quickly and nearer to me than before. Finally, there was one final push and what or whomever it was rushed up beside me, came around until it was in my face, and was gone.

My friend, beside me the whole time, never heard or felt a thing. She's a medium and asked if I felt drawn to a particular area. I actually did. It was to two graves diagonally across from each other; both belonging to men named Henry. I never had any other experiences there, but to this day, whenever I pass by, I call out to my Henrys and wave. – *Lisa J.*

## Not Entirely Abandoned

I recently went on a ghost hunt at an abandoned asylum. I was in a jail cell and touched the bedframe. Instantly, I became sad and cold and had to leave. A bit later, I returned and while standing in the doorway of the cell, one of the guys asked a question. The answer was a bang either on the bedframe or the radiator behind me, from the inside of the cell. Whatever it was, was in the room with me. Shortly after, all activity was down the hall. It left me. But, in feeling this spirit I was thinking that it should use my energy. It sure as hell did that! That was a weird experience. – *Michael V., Pennsylvania*

## An Antique Mirror

When my daughter was about five or six years old, we were gifted an antique bed set complete with a mirrored dresser. It always gave off a weird vibe. I used to cover the mirror at night for her because it gave her the creeps.

One night, while I was reading her a story, the power in her room went out. JUST her room. We removed the mirror and put it in the garage. The activity in her room stopped. We had the mirror cleansed, but it still had a negative feel and we ended up selling the entire bed set. – *Cari F.*

## Highlights of My Haunted History

I've been a sensitive since I was a little girl and I've lived in the oldest, still-standing house in our town…with five spirits. The first was an old man. I don't know his name, and no one knows who he is. He would walk behind me a lot but only upstairs. In one of the bedrooms, he would tuck you into bed for the night. He loved to play his music, which sounded like Little House on the Prairie-type music, but on Sundays we'd hear church-type organ music. For the record, we didn't have a TV or any radios as we lived in such a remote area.

The next spirit was Dottie. She was a previous owner who died in the house in the early 1990s, in what became my bedroom. Every night, as soon as I lay down in bed and turned out the light, she would walk into the room, go around the bed to the door and walk out. I would see her shadow.

The spirits of three children also reside in the house. They were between the ages of four and nine years old and died in 1781 from what is now known as strep throat. We'd hear marbles drop and roll across the floor, and later find them. We'd watch the old door latches jiggle. The sound of little footsteps was heard constantly coming from upstairs. The three are buried on the property along with what we believe to be many other bodies. The home, built in the mid-1700s, has passed through quite a few generations. A friend of mine brought a metal detector to check out the area and found musket balls, period jewelry, etc.

I believe one of the children went home with one of my

granddaughters. Out of the blue, she was talking about the friend who was with her now.

There is actually a sixth spirit on the property, but she is in the barn. While I lived there, I had about 120 chickens, ducks and turkeys, and when I would go into the barn, I was always greeted by a woman's voice saying, "Good morning!" It was not Dottie.

When I was little, maybe about five or six years old, my aunt and my mother played with a Ouija board. They were trying to contact dead relatives. After that, things didn't feel right in the house, and I believe they let something "not so nice" in. Dresser drawers would open and close, as would doors. I would hear my name called – inside the house - by my mom and I'd look only to see her outside at the other end of the yard. My brother would feel hot air on his neck and hear a grunting in the corner of the bedroom. More than once, I had my wrist grabbed and I'd be pulled upright at 3:13 a.m.

1990. I was about five months pregnant and would get up to make my husband breakfast at 5:00 a.m. He'd leave for work, and I would go back to bed. We were planning a camping trip in Maine. That morning, I got back into bed, and I heard him calling my name. I hadn't heard any sounds of the doors opening or closing, no footsteps of him coming back into the house. Something didn't seem right. I leaned to look into the hallway.

Standing there was a woman in a tan trench coat, black gloves and a kerchief. She had no face and no lower body! I had never been so scared. I scrambled to climb out the bedroom window, called my girlfriend and had her come pick me up. I didn't go back into the house until we returned from Maine.

When we went back, my mother was mad. She said, "You think you're funny, don't you?"

I asked, "What?"

"You got them out of the bag."

"Mom, I don't know what you're talking about."

We went inside and I followed her into her room. Laid out on her bed were the trench coat, gloves and kerchief. They were my aunt's clothes. She passed away in 1976.

Fast forward to a Halloween night at Ed and Lorraine Warren's Occult Museum. We heard them speak, took a tour of Union Cemetery and then were able to walk through their museum in Monroe, Connecticut. I remember we had to sign waivers before going in to state that we wouldn't touch anything. If you don't know about their museum, it contains objects removed from various haunted locations to keep the residents safe. Many are said to contain negative entities and evil attachments. The real Annabelle doll is housed there in a glass case.

I asked if I would be allowed to take photos and they said yes, but absolutely no flash photography. I took four pictures of Annabelle. All turned out normal, but the fourth photo shows the Raggedy Ann doll with glowing red eyes. Remember, I hadn't used a flash. I sent the photo to the Warrens.

Lorraine called me. "Do you need the picture back?"

I let her know she could keep it. I had copies. I asked her why she thought it happened.

Her response? "Annabelle shows herself to people when she wants to."

On talking with Lorraine, I asked about my house. She said that something had been released during the Ouija use that was evil or demonic. As for the aunt's clothing and hubby's voice, she said she thought something was trying to latch onto my child.

I met my boyfriend in 2005. He was a skeptic with regard to the paranormal and my sensitivities. He and his friend decided to take me to Richmond, Rhode Island, one night to the smallpox village – it was a hospital camp in the woods where people had been sent to die. Hundreds of people are buried there.

As we drove through in the jeep, I could see people in the tree line wearing era style clothes, but as we went along, I kept seeing one particular little girl. She was wearing a white dress with a blue bow and had blonde hair. No shoes, and maybe five or six years old. At every twist and turn of the road, at every bend, she would be standing in the middle of the road, staring at me, about 200 feet ahead. This went on for about an hour. I told my boyfriend, "The little girl is coming home with me." He didn't believe it.

When we got to a part of the drive where there were two straight rows of extremely tall pines, I said, "Get us out of here NOW." It felt like there were thousands of hands trying to get into the vehicle, and they were angry.

One day shortly after that, my two oldest children went off to school and my youngest, just four years old, was home with me. I heard my daughter chattering away and asked her who she was talking to. She said, "My new friend Leah." I let her know that I couldn't see her friend, and she told me that Leah had died "a long time ago in the woods." From then on, I couldn't see the little girl anymore, but my daughter could.

Leah stayed in our home for nearly four years when my mother started saying she would see a little girl at the end of her bed, smiling at her. A week and a half later, Mom was diagnosed with breast cancer and leukemia. When Mom passed, Leah left. None of us saw her again after that.

After my oldest was in the high school marching band parade at Disney World, my brother was coming home with her. They got off the plane and my daughter stopped abruptly to bend down for something. She picked up a bracelet with little letters on it. They spelled out "Leah."

Over time we researched some old historical books and found a picture of the doctor in charge of the smallpox village. Standing in front of him was his daughter, with blonde hair, in a little white dress and blue bow. Her name was Leah.

I believe that Leah somehow knew my mother was going to be ill and pass, and she stayed with us until it was time. She was there to help my mother pass over and then left with her.

Now when my mom passed away, she was eighty-five. She and my dad had been married nearly fifty years, but my dad had died seven years earlier. Mom would always say, "I miss Dad. I want to be with Dad." As time progressed and she was closer to her own death, she asked, "What if Dad doesn't come meet me? What if he found a new girlfriend in Heaven?"

I told her, "Mom, it doesn't work like that."

We were all sitting there with her and asked, "Will you do us a favor?"

"What?"

"When you pass and Dad comes to meet you, will you give us a sign that Dad was there to greet you?"

I have to say, within about fifteen seconds of her taking her last breath, every smoke alarm in our mother's house went off and all the pots and pans started banging.

Additionally, I have my mother's music box that she picked up in Germany on her European trip. It has to be opened in order to play. The song is Edelweiss. I have it in my bedroom and there are many times when music started playing without it being opened. Also, I had a huge wall mirror over the sink in my bathroom. There were a few times I walked into that bathroom, and I could see my mom standing behind me, smiling.

A side note on my parents' house. When the field was plowed, they found arrowheads, clay marbles, etc. My two youngest refused to sleep at their nan's as they said a man with "long white hair and feathers down to his feet" was very mean. They said he would yell at them, but they didn't know what he was saying. They also mentioned a boy with black hair, a feather and a dog who would always wake them up.

Another time, my boyfriend was renovating a house and brought something home. Something unseen. Our cat was inside, on the couch when we went to bed. When my boyfriend got up early the next morning to go to work, he wanted to know why I had left the cat outside all night. He said she was crying to come in. The last I had seen she was inside, and I hadn't let her out.

Next, my daughter was complaining that I had left the door to her rats' cage open, and her three rats were loose in her room. I hadn't done that, either.

The following day, I was home alone and every door in the house slammed shut at once. I stood up and yelled, "I don't know who you are. I don't know where you came from. You are not welcome here. You are disrupting my family. You need to go! You do not belong here! You need to get out!"

It went. We weren't bothered by it again.

When we moved to an apartment in Providence, it felt wrong. This was something that I call a tormentor. It would sit at the base of the bed and bounce up and down. My boyfriend sensed it, but it never happened when he was in bed. Only me. We would be sitting in the TV room and pots and pans would hit the floor in the kitchen.

One night my boyfriend went to work, and I was all by myself. I was vacuuming in the TV room. Up until that day, it never came into that room. It would stay in the "L" shaped part of the apartment. But that day, I felt it come right up on me – to my back. I shut off the vacuum and dropped it, grabbed my pocketbook and cell phone, and went next door. My boyfriend's best friend lived in the next apartment. I told him I couldn't go back home until my boyfriend was there. This torment went on for almost a year.

Our friend next door was supposed to get heart surgery and developed complications. My boyfriend always walked his dog in the morning and evening to help him out. We both had a key to his place. I would clean and do the dishes for him. When he got sicker, he asked if my boyfriend would continue to walk his dog for him. He and my boyfriend would have coffee together at 6:00 a.m. each day. It was their morning ritual.

One morning, my boyfriend told me he thought our friend was still sleeping. Hours went by. I needed to go to the laundromat, but before I left, I stopped directly across from our front door. This put me against the wall of our friend's bedroom. If we knocked on his front door, he wouldn't hear it. We would knock on the bedroom wall to let him know when we were there. I could hear him in his bedroom. He was a big burly guy and had a distinct laugh. He seemed to be giggling and laughing, so I figured he was okay. I went to the laundromat.

When I returned, I told my boyfriend he needed to go check on our friend. "Maybe he needs to go to the doctor or something."

He left and came running back screaming, "He's dead! He's dead!"

I ran over. It was the middle of August, and about 100 degrees outside. I tried to get a pulse, find a breath, but he was ice cold. Rigor mortis was already setting in.

We called the police who contacted the coroner. After he examined our friend, I asked him, "Can you roughly tell me about what time he passed away?"

"Oh, definitely pre-dawn. Full rigor mortis has already set in." Full rigor takes approximately six to eight or more hours.

"You're f***ing lying."

"Um, no. I've been doing this over thirty years and no, this was full rigor mortis, and my time stamp is before the sun came up this morning."

I said, "Bullsh*t. Because I heard him in his bedroom around noon, giggling and laughing."

"Do you want to know why you heard him giggling and laughing?"

"No."

"He didn't want you to be the one to find him."

A couple of weeks passed by and this thing in our apartment was still active. I was standing in the doorway of the bathroom, talking to my boyfriend in the TV room and I felt this huge hand on my shoulder – pushing down enough to where my shoulder slipped off the door jam. I felt peace. I said, "Okay." I knew it was our friend who had passed away, letting me know he was still around. And, after that happened, the thing in the apartment never bothered us again.

But! . . . the landlord wanted my boyfriend to tear up the carpet and put in laminate flooring. Right in that doorway where I said that thing would never cross, we found a huge, dried blood spot on the floor. They never cleaned it up, just covered it with the carpet. Whoever died in that apartment was still there – till our friend passed away. I think he either chased it out or kept it under control.

Yet another time, I was at a coworker's picnic and a lady I didn't know approached me. "Can I talk to you?" she asked.

I'm a friendly person, so I said, "Sure."

"Who's the little boy?"

I didn't know who she was talking about. "What do you mean little boy? I don't see any little boy."

The woman said, "No, no, no. On the other side, Hon. He's standing on the side of two men in uniform."

Now I lost a son in 1986 at birth. When we buried our son, we had a huge family plot. My father was the youngest of nine; I'm the youngest of six. A big family and we had a large section of the cemetery. The funeral director had said to my dad, "Why are we going to make you spend the money on a plot for the baby when we can bury him between your two brothers?" My uncles had both served in the military. So, my son was beside two men in uniform. I always believed my uncles were watching over him.

This woman knew things about me and my family she couldn't possibly know. But she did.

One of the most memorable experiences happened six years ago. My best friend in the world, O.D., (everyone called him O.D. as he didn't like his name) passed away at the age of forty-nine. I had been sitting at a fire when my phone rang. It was his mother. "I have sad news," she said. "O.D. passed in his sleep last night from a massive heart attack." I was stunned. He had no health issues and now my closest friend was gone.

One night three months later, my daughter came running out of her bedroom. "Mommy! There's a man's face on my wall!" She had been playing on Snapchat, taking pictures. She showed me the picture and I about fell backwards in my chair. My kids had never met O.D., but it was him in the picture. I could make out his features easily in the blur of light on her wall.

My daughter said, "Mom, what's the matter?"

After I had recovered, I opened my phone and showed her a picture of O.D.

"Mom. Who's that?"

"My friend, O.D. You've heard me talk about him many, many times, but you've never met him."

"Yeah, you talk about him all the time." As she looked at the photo, she said, "Mom. That's the same guy."

"I know."

About four years ago, I had rotator cuff tears and needed an MRI, which is very hard for me because I'm extremely claustrophobic. Well, I was in the machine like a sardine, and I started to hyperventilate. I was going to have a panic attack when the lady said to me, "What kind of music do you like?"

"Classic rock, 80s rock…"

She put the music on for me and the very first song was I Don't Wanna Miss a Thing by Aerosmith, which happened to be O.D.'s and my favorite song. The second that song came on, I calmed right down. I knew he was there with me.

When I had the surgery, while I was under anesthesia, I could see him and my parents as clear as day. They were telling me, "You're going to be fine. Everything's going to be okay." It was as if they were standing right in front of me. I knew I would be fine.

A final remarkable experience happened when I was visiting with my girlfriend. She lived in one half of a duplex, and we were sitting out on the stone wall smoking a cigarette. I looked up at her daughter's bedroom window. I knew her daughter was at a sleepover at a girlfriend's house.

"You didn't tell me you had company. I got you out here and you've got company. There's an old man up in Jessie's room."

She said, "I have no company."

"Well, there's an old man in your daughter's bedroom."

"Explain him to me."

I described exactly what he looked like. Prior to this, I had told her there was somebody in her daughter's bedroom because, even in the middle of August with no air conditioning, that room was always cold.

She said, "You just described my pépé. My pépé built this house."

"Well," I said. "I'm guessing that's who I saw."

She brought me into the house and pulled out an old picture of a group of people. There had to be twenty or more in the photo of those who belonged to the French club in town. "Out of this picture, I want you to point out who you saw in the window."

I saw him right away and pointed.

"That's my pépé!"

He's there, watching over her daughter. – *Cathy G.*


## Move Over . . .

One time I was lying in bed and just falling asleep when my bed was shoved and a man said, "HEY," in my ear. I thought maybe I was on the verge of sleep and tried to go back to sleep. It happened again! I could sense someone in bed behind me. I reached back and felt a man's fingers. I've never flown out of bed so fast! – *Tamara, California*


## Utter Grief

Last Friday, my children's stepfather took his own life. Sunday evening, he came to me in my sleep, looking scared, sad and confused. Monday morning, I could feel his presence with me as I worked. I could smell him. I felt a presence behind me, that of a child hiding behind their parent. Behind me and off to the side. He stayed with me all day. I talked to him. I comforted him and let him know what had happened, and that he was welcome to stay with me as long as he needed to. I also told him that he needed to sit with our youngest daughter and his wife. Tuesday, I didn't feel him.

Today, he was with me at work and on my car ride to the car dealership. I can feel him and still smell him. It's not scary or anything at all. It's very sad and heartbreaking. But as I write this, I can sense him sitting next to me. I do think he spends most of his time at his house, though, as I go there often to help out with chores and to pick up the kids.

I had taken some empty boxes down to their basement, which is where he died, and I felt immediately ill and dizzy. Not a sensation that I've experienced before, but I think it was because he met his end right there that he was very strong in that room.

I had also sensed him when I mowed their – his – lawn . . . and felt him walking behind me and had this uncomfortable feeling that I was doing it wrong. I think he was upset that I was there doing these things. But I talked to him, out loud, and told him that I was doing these things for the kids. I wasn't there for her. When I told him that, the feeling of dread seemed to dissipate, and I was able to finish mowing their grass. – *Nathan B., Kentucky*

## An Investigation at Craig Y Nos

As a team, we were investigating Craig Y Nos Castle in Wales. This is a very old, stunning building. We explored various rooms from the new refurbished to the old, dilapidated ones.

The one place I was truly fascinated with was the theatre. There is a long hallway leading to the theatre separated by two double doors. We split up to cover more ground on the investigation. I took the hallway and theatre.

Everything went still. Quiet. I was asking for something to happen, movement, a voice, anything. A chill started at my neck and traveled down my back. I also felt I was not alone and was being watched, but I could see no one.

I started taking photographs all around me. Nothing was captured. I had the feeling I should take photographs of the double doors. The back double door, the left-hand side door, was open. The front double door, the right-hand side door was open. This left a gap of darkness in between the doors.

I took one photograph and the feeling of being watched intensified. I looked quickly at the photograph I had taken and there, staring back at me, was a face in between the gap in the doors.

I ran to the doors and looked through. Nothing was there. I searched the theatre. Behind the curtain and stage...nothing.

Comparing the photo to the previous owner, I was surprised to find such a similar face staring back at me.

To this day, when I visit Craig Y Nos, it never disappoints. I have had many experiences there since like voices, singing and music when the place had been totally empty.

I feel a massive honour to have been allowed to witness this event and for the previous owner to allow me to see her. – *Tressa Yeomans, Rugeley Supernatural Society*

## He Walked Right Through Me

I had an experience when I was seven years old going to visit a lonely old lady in Tonawanda. Her husband had been an alcoholic and abusive. They found him dead one morning from fumes from an old, big stove. That happened in the late 1800s. It was claimed she did it, but she told me he forgot to light the stove before he passed out. She said he would come back to visit her and if I saw him not to be scared.

Well, he did. I sat on the porch, and I heard someone walking around the corner, right up to me and walked through me into the house. Never saw him but when he got in front of me, he stopped for a second...like he saw me...and went right through me into the house.

I never went back. – *Maxi D.*

# His Old Room

One time when I was around ten years old, we visited my grandparents and I had to sleep in a room where my mama's stepbrother had committed suicide. During the night I woke up and felt pressure on the bed behind me, like someone sat down. It scared me to the point I was afraid to breathe. I finally drifted back to sleep. I'll never forget it. – *Guina S., Alabama*

# A Slap in the Face

Years ago, I'd say I was age six to seven, I'd be asleep in my own room when I'd feel a slap against my face. I'd wake up and see nothing. Everybody was sleeping in their rooms and the family pets sensed nothing. This went on for a while until we got new bedroom furniture. I never told anyone in the family this as they wouldn't have believed me. I'm not sure why I was targeted but know that spirits can have attachments to things.

We were the fourth owners of the house, I think, and I was told that the original owner and my godfather both passed on the property. – *James R., Pennsylvania*

# An Old Friend's Passing

Several weeks ago, someone who I haven't seen or heard from in over thirty-five years, popped into my head. I wondered how he was doing and if he married the woman he was so in love with. (He left a job to be with her).

On Saturday night, I walked into my bedroom and went around the bed to turn on the power strip. Something touched me above my upper lip. Of course, I thought it was some sort of bug. I checked the ceiling, walls and even crawled under my bed. Nothing was found!

I turned the TV on and was watching a show when, out of the corner of my right eye, I saw a small, almond shaped, cream-colored light. It dissolved when it went by. Again, I started to look for bugs. There was nothing there to create or mimic that small light. Nothing was found, again! All of a sudden, "someone died" or "was going to die," popped into my head.

The next morning, Sunday, when I read the paper, I saw that the man whose name had been in my head several weeks before, DIED!! Did I somehow sense that I was going to see his name in the future?! Was he touching me to let me know he was on the other side? I did realize that the touch and orb were from him, and I did thank him. I hope to see him on the other side! – *Jane K., Pennsylvania*

## A Head Wound

My experience happened in Gettysburg, Pennsylvania. The Lightner Farmhouse, to be exact. The Lightner is a bed and breakfast now. During the Civil War it was a Union hospital. We had just returned from a tour on the battlefields and the tour continued at the B&B.

We left the carriage house/triage and were headed toward the orchard, when something stopped me in my tracks. I couldn't move. I couldn't see and I was starting to shake. My husband asked if I was okay and, crying, I managed to get out, "No. I'm not."

Our guide turned, grabbed my arm and said, "Get her out of that spot!"

After being moved, I started to regain my senses. When we left the next day, I noticed myself constantly rubbing my forehead. It felt like there was a bandage around my head. – *Pamela S., Arkansas*

## Time to Make the Bed

When I was about six years old, I was trying to fall asleep at my step grandmother's house in Hesperia, California. The room I was in was ALWAYS the coldest in the house. I was dozing off when my blankets folded back in a perfect triangle, and I felt someone sit on my bed. I screamed. They got up and it never happened again. But that room remained the coldest in the house. – *Cari F.*

## Grandma's Perfume

My grandmother, who was like my mother, died of cancer when I was seventeen years old. I was pregnant with my first child, who was due in late October. My grandmother passed over in early July. I was already emotionally distressed from being pregnant, and my grandmother's death made it even harder for me.

One day, about two months after my daughter was born, I was sitting on my bed writing poetry, sad, and in my feelings. All of a sudden, I smelled a familiar fragrance. It was the perfume that my grandmother wore. Out of nowhere, I had the feeling of someone standing behind me; I spun around and there was no one there. I was so freaked out that I left my daughter lying on the bed and ran to my mother's room. I told her everything that had happened. She looked at me and said, "Oh, that was just mother coming to see you and the baby." …but grandmother is dead…!! – *Teresa H., Wisconsin*

## Stopped in His Tracks

My brother bought an old farmhouse that hadn't been lived in for thirty-five years and needed a ton of renovations. We spent months getting the home ready and one day we were up on the roof, shingling. I was walking across the peak of the house when I tripped.

I fell and hit the porch roof at a run, trying to catch my footing. Stumbling toward the edge, I could hear my brother screaming for me.

Just before I went over the edge, I was stopped short.

My brother yelled, "What happened?"

I turned. Eyes wide, heart pounding. "Someone threw their arm across my chest. I felt the arm!"

Someone kept me from falling off the porch roof that day. I don't know who but am grateful. This wasn't the first, or last, experience at that house. — *Randy S., New York*

# 4

# ONLY IN YOUR DREAMS...
# OR IS IT?

We've all had dreams that seemed as tangible and intense as real life. Perhaps you've had a real heart to heart with someone who's crossed over and swore when you woke that it had to have happened. Or you've dreamed of a tragic accident, only to read about it in the papers a week later.

In our dream states, we are more receptive to the "otherworldly" and unusual. Spirits have long used dreams to warn or protect, to announce...and even just to prove the reality of their existence.

And, sometimes, their warnings cross over to the waking state. Precognition and premonition can take place while asleep or awake but are they intuition based or messages from beyond the grave? You be the judge.

In the fall of 1982, I dreamed that my mother and I were in my middle sister's home. Mom was seated on the sofa, with a soft light coming through the windows. I was sitting on the floor when my sister walked into the room. Mom told us that she had cancer and was terminal. The shock of what she said woke me. I was in tears, unable to shake a feeling of dread. The dream had been so vivid, the message so real, that I couldn't escape the upset the entire day. It was as if Mom had delivered the message herself and I was losing her.

Twelve years later, Mom found a lump in her breast and underwent an immediate mastectomy. Radiation and chemotherapy saved her life, and she was with us another twenty-one years. Did my mother warn us twenty years before? Was this coincidental and my own fears were incorporated into the dream, leading me to believe she was dying? I don't believe in coincidence.

1988 rolled around. My grandmother on Mom's side had passed away the prior May. I dreamed that I was going up an escalator in a mall. My grandmother was sitting on a bench at the top. She was wearing a brilliantly colored dress, brighter and more colorful than anything I'd ever seen before. I commented on it, and she said simply, "These are just some flowers that blew across my grave." I woke, stunned by the radiance of the flowers and my grandmother's off the cuff statement. She'd made her entrance. She had my attention.

Over the years, I had many dream visits with my grandmother. They took the form of us talking on the telephone or sitting at a picnic table and chatting. Or she'd be in the background in a gathering of people but would always take even a small part in my dreams. I asked her once why she was with me so much. Her answer? "I'm watching over the children." As much as I enjoyed her being around, and believed she was with me in spirit, I still questioned on some level if she was *really* there each night. That changed in the winter of 1997.

The setting of the dream was the basement of my mother's house. My mother and grandmother were having a discussion... about what, I don't know. My grandmother told me that Hans, Mom's dog, was dead. Mom said she already knew, but I wasn't believing it. The calendar in front of me read April. I tried to turn the pages back to an earlier month because the timing felt wrong. But the pages wouldn't change. The feeling I got was that you can't turn back time or stop the event. It was inevitable. I woke believing that Hans would die in either April or August, a month beginning with A.

Hans died in August.

Was my grandmother warning me? Announcing the event? Or was she establishing that our dream communication was real, and validating her visits? I believe she wanted to rid me of my questions and prove her presence was real.

June of 2013 brought with it more "proof." It was early morning, and I was dreaming that I was going to the store with my parents and grandmother. I was driving Mom's car late that night. I turned on the headlights, but they were very dim. Nearly out. I was struggling to see and working hard to keep the car on the road. There weren't even streetlights to help guide me.

When we finally pulled into the parking lot of a store, it was well lit. I noted the contrast of darkness to an extremely well-lighted area and appreciated that we could now see. We walked around the convenience store for a few minutes and waited for Mom and my grandmother to get a snack. My dad and I found a picnic bench for them to sit while they ate.

My grandmother sat across from me, looking thirty years younger than when she died. Vibrant! She was happy and joking, smiling the entire time. All at once, she was beside me. She said, "I look at all dreams as a warning."

I passed it over, concentrating on our original conversation, and she said, again, "I look at all dreams as a warning."

When I woke, I took the message to heart and checked my car. One of the headlights was indeed out. I got the bulb changed and thanked my grandmother for letting me know.

Sometimes the messages we get may be necessary, but that doesn't make them any easier. In June of 2015, I dreamed that I was at Mom's house once again. There were a lot of people milling around. My grandmother was there. Mom was getting ready to go somewhere, and my sister had set up her oxygen tank. I picked it up to check it and made sure it was set correctly. Mom said she wanted to talk to us when everyone else was gone. She told me, "It's okay if I go. It's not a problem if I go." Mom passed away six months later.

Not long after she died, I dreamed that my phone was ringing. I grabbed it and swiped to answer the call. Instead of coming up with a name or number, my phone's screen had the picture of a key. (The night before I had been setting up my new laptop and made an icon for a paranormal file...a gold key).

When I answered the call, my dad said hello and handed the phone to Mom. She started talking and laughing, telling me how much she was enjoying traveling...to New York, New Jersey, Pennsylvania and California. I corrected her, saying that she must've meant Connecticut since they were driving and we're on the east coast. She laughed and agreed with me. She sounded fabulously happy and twenty years younger. She was thrilled - it was so nice to be out and about again, without pain or having to carry an oxygen tank. My mind immediately went to...wait...who's driving? Mom can't see to drive, and Dad has dementia... and he can't possibly be out and about like that as he's been living with my oldest sister since Mom passed away. My mind was racing as my alarm went off, but I woke with the knowledge that Mom is taking Dad traveling in his dreams.

The most serious warning I received didn't come in a dream.

August 2017. Some of the members of Sullivan Paranormal (my investigating team) were with me at my mother's house. Mom passed away in December 2015 and we had gotten into the habit of using her home for our meetings while I fixed it up to sell.

It was a comfortable, peaceful place where we could plan our investigations. We had been on Skype chatting with a radio host about a potential interview on his program and when we were done, we relaxed for a bit. As we sat talking, we decided to do a mini-investigation since it was quiet and seemed like we weren't alone in the house. Quite a few people had asked me over the past year and a half if I would ever investigate my mother's house and it finally felt okay. Mom wouldn't have minded.

I had to drive home to pick up the equipment we wanted. I noticed my mother in the passenger seat beside me. She gently laid her hand over mine on the steering wheel and kept repeating, "It's coming. It's coming." This was the only thought in the forefront of my mind, over and over.

I walked inside and let my husband know what we were doing. He'd had a few drinks and we got into a conversation on his views on death, specifically my mother's. She'd died at home, in her sleep, and he felt she probably waited around for a day or two and then, metaphorically, "got her wings" before moving on. It wasn't what I believed, as she was still coming around, but we chatted a little. He seemed fixated on her getting "wings."

When I returned to Mom's, we set up the equipment in her bedroom. Only a voice recorder, Mel Meter and Ovilus. We weren't interested in setting up cameras, just in communication if Mom was around. I told the team about sensing her in the car and what she kept saying to me. We began the EVP session. Across the Ovilus came the words:

William

Strength

Wings

I proceeded to tell the girls about the conversation I had had with my husband when I picked up the equipment and we pondered what the message meant. Everything pointed to my father's impending death as he was in hospice at the time. His name was William.

We continued the session. I was at a loss for questions and asked Mom how she liked our trip to Virginia the previous month. I made the seven-hour drive to be with my dad on his ninety-first birthday. Mom, in spirit, was beside me for nearly the entire ride. The Ovilus gave the words:

Slower.

Trip

I had hit rush hour on the beltway around Washington, D.C., and it added an hour to the drive. It again confirmed that it was Mom who was with us in the room. Not that I doubted it with all that had been going on.

We kept the session short. It felt great to know that Mom was close, but bittersweet realizing that my dad wouldn't be around much longer.

Two days later my husband died. It never even crossed my mind that his name was also William. Mom tried to warn me.

## Warned . . . but Why?

I'm a nurse and had a patient who I took care of for two weeks prior to him getting his second cardiac bypass surgery. The night before he went, I had a dream that I told him not to let that doctor do his surgery that day. I told my boyfriend (at the time – now my husband) who was also a nurse. He worked in the heart surgical unit, where they first come out of cardiac surgery and stay for a few days, then go back up to my floor.

He said, "Oh, my God, you can't tell him that!"

I said, "I realize that!" But I was the one who had to get him ready to go, give him his meds, pack him up and send him off to the OR. I felt like an executioner sending someone to the gallows.

I called and told Chris (my boyfriend) that I was sending the patient down and to keep me posted. He called an hour or two later to tell me the patient coded on the table, but they got him back. I said, "Okay. Call me when it's over…"

Two hours later he called to tell me that the patient died on the OR table. I think that's when he really started to believe that I wasn't crazy, and I actually knew things before they happened. Not a great time to be a nurse! Things like this happened to me often. I was young and didn't know what to do with the knowledge. I had to pray it away. It's not my job to change someone's story. It's already written. But why am I seeing and knowing these things if I can't or shouldn't change them? – *Nora Jo M. L.*

# Step Up

I was on a stage in high school waiting for play rehearsal to start. I was talking to someone across from me when I heard a voice whisper, "Step up," in my left ear. I stepped forward. The strip of stage lights weighing hundreds of pounds fell directly behind me in the spot where I had been standing. I would have been killed had I not "stepped up." – *Valerie Y.*

# Marked

I started a new relationship with a man about four years ago. I live in and am from the Midwest. He is from Virginia. While getting to know each other, he mentioned his grandmother being a witch who lived in the Appalachian Mountains. I totally thought he was trying to one-up my stories of neglect, foster care and abandonment issues. I had never heard of such nonsense, passed it off as such and had a good chuckle. A little while later, we moved to another home in another state and were starting our lives together.

We awoke one bright sunshiny morning and realized it was way too early to get up on our day off from work. So, we cuddled and fell back to sleep. As quickly as I fell asleep, I woke back up, or so I thought. I looked at the doorway and noticed a little old lady crouched down, dressed in all black. I ignored her and hoped I was having a bad dream and she'd go away. But she didn't. She spoke to me as she scurried her way next to my side of the bed. She said, "I am tired of you ignoring me."

"I am sorry," I replied. "I didn't realize you were here for me."

"I have been waiting a long time to talk to you."

I used to drink quite often but that particular night before I did not. She didn't give me a chance to respond. She started in on me, claiming I treated her grandson horribly. I felt verbally attacked and misunderstood. I immediately defended myself.

"Why does he lie so much and about almost everything?" I felt she knew what I was talking about (his kids, his finances). I was telling her it's hard to build a solid relationship on lies. The discussion was escalating as we were both trying to make valid points, then I heard him yelling really loudly.

"Hey! Wake up!"

I wanted to finish explaining to her, so I tried to ignore him. I looked away from him and back to her, but before I could talk or move, she lunged toward me and bit the knuckles of my left hand. I was very confused, and upset, about the bite. He succeeded in waking me up and making her disappear. I thought I had been awake, so I was not understanding why he said, "You were having a bad dream." He seemed very concerned and a little frightened. He said I was speaking in a language he never heard before, and in a voice he'd never heard me use. I was shocked and didn't know what to think.

"What were you dreaming about?" he asked.

I simply said, "I met your grandmother."

"What did she say? Was she mad?"

I didn't feel like talking about our encounter right away. I didn't know how to process the whole thing.

A few weeks later I told him everything from beginning to end and asked, "Why did she bite me?!"

He acted like it was no big deal and said he didn't want to tell me because I looked mad. I said, "Well, WTF does it mean? Am I going to die soon?!"

He said, "No. She just marked you for me."

I am still not 100 percent sure what that means, but here we are a few years later and I think now I am mostly surprised he told me the truth about something from his past. And yes, I have since seen, and heard, the YouTube stories about Appalachian witches. – *Sarah M., Kansas*

# Heed the Warning

When I was little, I was a very heavy sleeper. My grandmother said one night I rose up on the bed, still asleep, arms pointing toward the living room screaming, "The house is on fire!" She went outside and saw that the breaker box was sparking. – *Jessica K., South Carolina*

# The "Hurt" Card

When I was about seventeen years old, I would often play hide and seek at a place we called "the cold house." We would also investigate this property very thoroughly over the course of a year and a half, and the encounters we had and the things we discovered were absolutely amazing.

For a little background to the property, we were checking the place out in the daytime. The house was a two-story, with the bedrooms upstairs. It had a pretty scary cellar, where I once saw two red glowing eyes, but that's a story for another time.

We headed upstairs, and I was the last one up, so I know that other than dirt and leaves, nothing was on the stairs. We checked out the two bedrooms and decided to go look at the back of the property. I led the way down the stairs and, about seven steps down (halfway down), directly between my feet, was a flashcard of sorts that said "HURT" in the middle of it. I picked it up and inspected it, looking for a manufacturer or something but, other than the word, the card was blank. I thought it was funny and took the card home.

I had a mini "altar" and on it I had a Ouija board. I laid the card on the corner of the board. The next day I was getting ready for school. Next to my bedroom door is a dresser with a vanity mirror and I was standing there, straightening my hair. My fan was on low because it was summertime; my room was upstairs, and it was super-hot up there. It also had a fairly high ceiling.

Suddenly, one of the blades of my fan went flying past my head and crashed into the mirror, breaking it into a million pieces. My mother and I were both pretty freaked out. I took that card and drove back to the cold house. I tore the card up and threw it into the ditch behind the property.

Flash forward about six weeks. I was helping my then boyfriend clean out his car. We were dumping the trash and I had the passenger seat forward to clean behind it. I picked up a bunch of trash and, underneath it all, laying perfectly on the mat was a card that said "HURT." I got pretty upset and held it up, demanding what it was.

"That's the card you found at the house a few weeks ago," he said to me.

"No, it's not," I said, and proceeded to tell him what I did with the card. He and I were both freaked out and could not explain it. My friends could've been messing with me but seeing the fear on his face that day told me otherwise.

Flash forward another few weeks and we were into the end of October, nearing Halloween. My boyfriend and I, as well as two other guys, decided to go play hide and seek out at the cold house. We played a few rounds and decided on one more before we hit the road. My boyfriend and his buddy, Justin, were on a team, and they were hiding. I was on a team with our friend Matt, and we were, obviously, seeking. We were at the back of the property counting while they hid.

When we started hunting them, we were on the outside of the barbed wire fence that surrounded the house. We could see them kind of hunched over and running toward the front of the property as we were crouched about halfway between the road and the house outside of the property line.

My friend hit my arm and said, "Who's that?"

I looked and saw a man in all black. He had a black wide brimmed hat and a black "cowboy-like" duster. We couldn't see his feet or face. We watched him walk toward the house from the road.

When he got closer to the house, we realized he wasn't walking. He was floating. He floated up the four steps into the house and disappeared. We took off running toward the car and honked the horn like crazy until the others came running. We left there so fast and explained what we had seen. They didn't see anything and were completely freaked out by what we had experienced! – *Kristin D., Colorado*

## Two Dreams of Death

While I was at college, I had a dream that my cat walked away into the woods, never to return. Days later, my mother called to let me know that my cat had disappeared. We never saw her again.

In December 1987, I had an incredibly realistic dream in which I was attending a funeral. I saw my grandmother, who had died the previous May, lying in an open coffin. She sat up and told me definitively that the funeral was not hers, but that of my Uncle John. My mother called me the next morning to let me know that my uncle had passed away. – *Susan C., Maryland*

## Life Changed in a Moment

These "dreams" led to my sobriety. I was asleep. My mind was clearing a bit from the alcohol. I was a mess, afraid, confused, depressed, lost, suicidal and miserable. I was at the shore, somewhere in New Jersey, either Wildwood or Sea Isle City. The houses all looked the same. I was drunk in this dream and only days into my half-sobriety. I say "half" because I was still drugging, just not drinking. But the "dreams" also led me to total sobriety.

I walked into a house and noticed it wasn't the one I had rented. I was standing in the living room, confused and crying. A woman came up to me. I can't help but think she was Mother Mary in the present. She asked if I was okay and wasn't upset a strange drunk man had entered her house. Nor was she afraid. I was in tears and apologized for being in the wrong house. She welcomed me inside and introduced me to her son. This is where it gets interesting. This lady's son was huge! He looked like a gentle giant with a baby face. He was wide in stature and looked to be very strong but also so very tender in his ways.

I remember the ceilings being very high, as well was this gentle giant, young boy-man. His eyes were as blue as the sea, so peaceful and forgiving. So childlike yet so angelic. This young man-child saw the misery on my face and tears in my eyes and grabbed a hold of me, lifting me over his head. I remember thinking, "I'm going to hit the ceiling!"

I didn't. The higher he lifted me, the more I felt guilt and misery melt away.

The next thing I remember is floating above him. He had let go and I was afloat. It felt nothing like I have ever felt before, awake or asleep. I felt instantly well, and I was happy. Something changed in me at that moment. I woke. I was amazed. I felt good. I started going to AA meetings and did everything I was told to do. I worked the step and continue to do so. This "dream" was the catalyst that led me to my newfound way of living. – *Michael V., Pennsylvania*

## Dreams of Death and Destruction

I receive "dreams" of those who are going to die. Several family members and friends have died in my dreams and the way they died in the "dream" was how they actually died. I had a dream of my cousin falling down steps and breaking something. I did not know the extent of her fall. I told my mom to relay the message to be careful around steps for a while. A few weeks later, my cousin fell down the steps and broke her hip. The message had never been relayed to her. Lesson learned. Never ask a person to deliver a message to someone else. Always do it yourself and try not to sound insane in telling them what you "saw."

I have "dreamed" of volcanoes erupting, earthquakes, war, devastation, death and blood. I've been in the middle of war and have seen what the future was going to be like. It is now as I saw it then. I've seen Benghazi destroyed when I didn't even know what a Benghazi was. Earthquakes would destroy cities in parts of the world, and I'd see it happen. I even saw myself hanging onto broken earth so as not to fall into a deep hole that would kill me, formed from an earthquake.

A couple of days later, I put on the news and saw what happened in my "dream" became a reality, minus me dying in it. I do not understand the parts where I am involved in the middle of war and destruction. I'm still figuring it out. And it's been years that I've been trying to understand how it all works.

I had a dream this past year about a friend with whom I no longer have contact. In this "dream," I was in the morgue with my friend's brother and my brother. There were three bodies on gurneys. I didn't see the boy but knew who it was. My friend passed away from a drug overdose. How I knew, I don't know. I just knew. The next day, since I couldn't warn my friend, I called his brother to relay the message to be careful of the drugs he was taking. He said he would tell him. I don't know for sure if he did or not, but shortly after he was supposed to have warned his brother, my friend went into rehab. He was discharged from rehab and went back to the drug of his choice. He is no longer with us. It took about a year and a half before this happened. Usually my "dream warnings" span from three days to a few weeks. But I am seeing some messages are for the deep future, much like my next.

Grim Reaper Dream. My cousin and I were walking down a narrow street, not in my neighborhood. There were iron gates in front of the houses. My cousin and I were walking along and talking. Let me tell you about my cousin. He walks hunched over from spinal surgeries done at a young age, but he was walking straight in this dream. I turned around and saw the Grim Reaper walking behind us.

Following us. We picked up the pace, walking quickly toward a house I didn't know. There were children playing in the front yard. It was a small, square yard with white iron rails. I called the kids inside, pushing them in. I was so afraid. We all got inside in the nick of time, or so I thought. His black sleeve went through the door with a scroll in his hand that read, in the middle of the scroll, 07-08-49. No list of names or other dates. Not even my name. Just the date. I woke. I'm still wondering and waiting on this date to see the outcome. I'm not sure if it pertains to me, personally, my death date, or if it's bigger than that. The end of the world? We shall see come 07-08-49. – *Michael V., Pennsylvania*

## A Sixth Sense

I've experienced paranormal things since the age of four. I used to see hooded figures and shapes. I would also tell my mother when a certain family member would die. She would get angry at me and tell me to stop. I continue to see dark figures and do have a sixth sense for things. – *Maura C.*

## A Chat with My Guardian Angel

Throughout my life, there have been many occasions where I probably should have, or could have, died. Dangerous situations I've put myself in, stupid decisions I've made and some just by the luck of the draw (and I don't believe in luck) have happened. And yet I've walked away unscathed.

One of the more recent experiences was when I was on my way home from work one evening when a driver leaving a convenience store confused the brake pedal with the gas and plowed into the front end of my Nissan Sentra. The car was totaled. I was fine. It happens, you say? Read on.

One afternoon I was mowing the grass at my mother's house, as I had for as long as I can remember. There is a slope to the ground as you get closer to the house and that day, I must've hit it at just the wrong angle. The tractor tipped backward and, with my weight anchoring it, flipped over. It rolled with the blades still turning and landed on my legs before coming to rest a few feet away. Shaking, I ran my fingers across the slice in my jeans. They were ruined but there wasn't even a scratch on my skin.

Another time, when I was younger, I went ice skating on a lake near my house. I skated there every winter, usually with my friends. It was getting a little late in the season and, for some reason, that day I went alone. I was a teenager and felt immortal.

The afternoon wore on and I was quite far away from the shore, at the other end of the lake, when I realized the sun was going down. It was dead quiet and going to be dark soon. As I began skating, I heard the crackling and snapping of ice breaking behind me. I knew I was in trouble and, if I went under, I would be in massive trouble. No one knew I was there, and it was too remote for anyone to find me if I couldn't get myself out of the water. I put my head down and skated for my life, as fast as I could, all the while knowing the path my skates were cutting was disintegrating. I finally reached the shore and sat down, panting. Safe.

Another winter, my girlfriend and I were driving home from college. I had been up late the night before, studying for a final, so she was driving my car. The weather had been iffy, but we headed home anyway.

On the highway, traveling about fifty-five miles per hour, my girlfriend panicked. She was boxed in, cars in front, to the left and behind, and the road was a sheet of ice. She had no control. The only thing in control of the car was momentum and that wasn't a good thing. She yelled, "Do something!"

Without hesitation, I grabbed the steering wheel and whipped it toward the right, hoping the wheels would grab some traction somewhere and take us in the only safe direction…off the road.

The next thing we knew, the car had spun around a few times, and we landed in about two feet of snow just past the shoulder. We sat, recovering, and watched as about twenty other cars spun, slipped and collided on that stretch of iced-over highway. We, however, were safe.

You might still argue that this is one incidence in a lifetime, but I'm telling you that, for whatever reason, whether it's "paranormal" or angelic, or both, I've been watched over. If I look back even farther, when I was about thirteen, my mother let me take her car to a friend's house. Yeah, it wasn't a great idea, but we lived out in the country on back roads, and it was a different time then. A time when kids could still ride in the backs of pickup trucks and such. I know, still not smart. But I did it and was excited about it.

My friends and I decided to go back to my house, and we piled into Mom's car, an old, maroon Monte Carlo. As I maneuvered the twists and turns of the road, one came on me fast and the car slid in the gravel. One of my friends yelled, "Hit the brake!"

Well, you can probably guess, I hit the gas.

We flew into the woods, barely missing a tree as a big rock under the car stopped us. Hard. Again, no one was hurt. Even the car, which had to be lifted off the rock and towed out of the bushes, was undamaged. Somehow. (And, no, I wasn't allowed to drive the car again for a very long time).

A few years prior to this, I was messing around with an oil lamp in my bedroom. Something startled me; it could have been my cat or my mother coming home, I don't remember. The lamp fell onto my carpet, igniting it. I beat out the flames with a towel. One more example of something that could have gone horribly wrong and didn't. Luck? Coincidence? I don't believe in either, at this point. My next, and the final experience that I will include here, is the most serious.

I was young. Eight or nine years old. My friend had come over to play and we ended up in my parents' bedroom. My father always kept a pistol in his nightstand, and I wanted to show it to my friend. I took the handgun out and, as we looked at it, it went off. I had pulled the trigger and blew a hole in the ceiling. My friend and I stood frozen in terror. I put the gun away and we went back to my room to process what had just happened. Again, an instance that could have gone terribly wrong, yet didn't.

In 2001, I had a "dream" where I met what had to be my guardian angel. It began in my old house, in the bedroom I had as a boy. A beautiful woman sat with me, and we talked for what seemed like the entire night. We even joked. I've never been so comfortable or happy in my life. She knew everything about me. I can't even describe the amazing feeling she brought...one of an all-encompassing peace. She told me that she is always with me and has always watched over me. She also said that she is a part of the unusual things that happen around me...like when I catch a light or movement out of the corner of my eye.

When I woke and realized it was "just a dream," I was thoroughly disappointed. I couldn't remember any of the details of the conversations we'd had and to be back in the "real world" felt empty. Like a loss. I know in my heart it wasn't a dream and that she was special beyond words. And that my experiences were more than just typical events in an everyday life. – *Liam O., New York*

## On Track

I had drinking dreams where I was drunk, and as the months and years went by, I would be at parties and not touch a drop of alcohol. In these "dreams" I would appear to be at parties with a deceased friend who passed away from alcoholism at an early age, in his twenties. In these dreams he is happy and not drinking where I, at first, would be drinking...to not drinking but wanting the drink...to not having the alcohol in front of me and not touching it. The same person was in these "dreams" over the years. It's been some time since I've seen him, but I remember him smiling at me without a glass of alcohol in my hand. Maybe that means that some of those who commit suicide or OD are in the same realm as others and not lost and alone. They seem to have some work to do before they can move on. My dead friend did a great job of helping me over the years. It's been fourteen years from 8/6/07.

Deeper in my sobriety, Mother Mary was in my backyard hovering over the garden with lilies on either side of her, also hovering in the air. No speech. I take it that it was a message that I was growing spiritually and on the right track. I seem to get these "on track/off track" messages in my "dreams." I love the "on track dreams!!" I've also dreamed of a saint I never heard of before. I looked him up and found him to be the Patron Saint of what I was going through at the time. Whatever issue that was, it turned out fine after that dream. He helped me along. I can't remember the name of this saint or what it was I was going through. I only remember looking him up and being awestruck comparing what I was going through to what he stood for. Simply amazing! – *Michael V., Pennsylvania*

## Antlers

Hi. My name is Maria M., and my story is about a death premonition I had in my dream. I have had many premonitions but I'm going to start with the most recent one that was about a year ago.

I fell asleep like I normally do, and the dream started with me, my boyfriend Lane, my roommate Chris and Chris' brother Austin, in the woods. We were walking with no clear direction and Austin was the only one with a gun. None of the rest of us had weapons. We got to a clearing and there was nothing but an open field with pine trees. It was quiet.

I started to cry, and Austin was the only one who noticed and asked what was wrong. Before I could answer, Lane and Chris pulled Austin down to the ground and told him not to move.

That's when I saw him. A tall male deer with huge antlers and no face. I asked him who he was.

In a deep voice he answered, "I am an ancient one." Trying not to cry, I asked him to let us leave but he said, "You go, they stay."

"Why?"

"You are a child of the land."

Those words still ring in my ears occasionally.

After he said this, I argued with him to let them go, too. He then sighed and said, "As you wish…but first…" he then whipped his head around and bit one of the guys. All I heard was a blood curdling scream before I blacked out in the dream. I woke up, still in the dream, in the hospital. Lane and Austin were crying, and their eyes were red. I went to look for Chris but when I pulled the curtain separating the room, I woke up in the real world. I was crying and hyperventilating and wondering what the hell happened. I began to fear for Chris' life because the last time I had a dream similar to this, someone died in real life with the same name as my roommate.

A few months went by, and I almost forgot my dream until a movie trailer came on TV…the trailer was for the movie Antlers. This story may not count as a death premonition, but it felt like a premonition none the less due to some of the similarities. I hope you guys enjoyed the story. – *Maria M., Ohio*

## A Motorcycle Warning

In September 1971, while living in Slidell, Louisiana, I had a premonition that I was going to be in a very bad motorcycle accident. The next day, a friend and I were riding our motorcycles. We stopped at a stop sign and there were a bunch of kids walking up the right side of the road with a truck coming up the side of the road toward us.

My friend and I left the stop sign at the same time. I sped up to get around him and he sped up, so I backed off to get behind him. I slowed and he slowed, swerving to miss the kids. I swerved to miss him.

I hit the truck head on.

I wound up crushing my left wrist and had a compound fracture of my left femur. The accident happened exactly the same as the premonition the night before. — *Matthew R., Oklahoma*

# 5

# WHAT WAS THAT?

Not everything tied to the spirit realm comes with a tidy explanation. Well, most of it doesn't. Some experiences, however, are more headscratchers than others. In this section, doppelgängers visit, an odd mist rises from a Ouija board and, I must admit, "Poke the Eyeball" has me a little creeped out. But let's begin with what I saw up in the woods one summer night…

It was August 2015. My niece and her family were visiting from Maryland. We were enjoying an end of summer camp out in the woods behind my house. There's a small trail that leads to a clearing with a firepit at the center. Their tents were set up; the kids were playing and, as the sun went down, we stoked a roaring campfire. Our chairs were arranged in a circle, the only sounds our voices, the snaps and pops of the flames and the settling of the forest into night.

As we sat talking and laughing, something caught my eye. I watched as a grapefruit-sized white sphere moved behind my niece and slowly up toward the trees. Then, it was gone.

I whipped around to try to see any light source, any beam or evidence that would explain or debunk what I had seen. The only light was the campfire in front of us. We were deep enough into my woods that my house wasn't visible from where we sat. Everyone was around the fire and pitch-black night surrounded us. Even a flashlight beam would have revealed itself as just that, and shone on the trees, rocks, and tent as it moved. This sphere emanated its own light.

I asked my niece, "Did you see that?"

Her eyes were wide, and she said she had. Twice. She first saw it a moment earlier...behind me...then as it moved up and away. Neither of us had an explanation for what we'd seen. I'm happy we both saw it, though. There's a lot to be said for validation.

Throughout the years, quite a few unusual experiences have also occurred inside my house. In July 2006, I noticed the smoke detector outside my bedroom door dangling from the ceiling. I ignored it, figuring my husband had been changing the batteries and would be back to finish soon. It was always a pain in the neck to deal with – you had to stand on a chair and wrestle with getting it back into its groove to twist it up into place. I forgot about it.

A few days later, when we returned from the county fair, my husband remarked how nice it was that I had fixed the detector. I looked up to see it was perfectly in place, screwed into the ceiling! I hadn't done it. The kids (then twelve, nine and seven years old) hadn't done it. They couldn't have reached it and had been with us the entire day. No one was home and no one had a key to the house. My husband said he hadn't touched it. Who screwed the smoke detector back into place? Obviously, someone wanted us to be safe...

When cleaning a couple of days later, I noticed that the little ceramic mouse my grandmother had painted many, many years before was turned backwards – facing the back of the shadow box. I had to climb on a chair and lean across the top of a bookshelf to turn it around. No one could have turned it; it was a struggle for me. And why would they have? Was this my grandmother letting me know that she had been in the house and fixed the smoke detector?

In February 2014, I was out picking up my oldest daughter from work. My husband and our younger children were home. When I returned, I opened the basement door to go upstairs and my dog, Mocha, greeted me. This was very unusual, and I thought that either she had rolled in something nasty and was put downstairs to wait for a bath, or my husband had heard me drive in and let her downstairs to greet me.

When I got upstairs, I called to my husband, "Why did you put Mocha in the basement?" I wasn't sure if maybe I should leave her down there or not.

"She's outside."

"She was in the basement when I walked in."

"That's not possible," he said. "I let her outside."

We always let her in and out through the front door, from the living room, upstairs. He told me he had been making our youngest a second bowl of noodles and heard Mocha bark to come in while he was in the kitchen.

"I called to her that she'd have to wait and went to fix the bowl of noodles. The next thing I knew, you were walking in." Our middle child was at the computer and our youngest was at the table eating. No one had let Mocha in. No one had put her into the basement. She couldn't have pushed the basement door open to let herself in (first of all, she waits at the front door to come inside, second of all, if she somehow HAD pushed the door open, she could not have pushed it shut…it closes hard). No neighbors live close enough to see our house, let alone bring the dog inside. Who put Mocha in the basement?

But one of my favorite experiences occurred on September 10, 2012. My oldest daughter had been bugging my husband off and on for a few months to get some of her old toys down from the attic. A friend of hers was having a baby and she thought something sweet and sentimental would make the perfect present.

The attic hatch is located at the end of the hallway near my children's bedrooms and there is a square board covering the opening. The ladder, an old wooden thing built specifically for this, is kept in the basement. We'd put the kids' beloved old toys in plastic bins with lids to keep them safe and stored them. It was a pain in the neck to lug the ladder upstairs as it was bulky, heavy, and rough to maneuver to get up to the crawlspace. The tubs were neatly stacked along one wall of the attic, out of the way.

Finally, my husband gave in and brought the ladder upstairs. Once it was positioned, he climbed up and positioned his hands to slide the board from the opening.

It didn't budge.

He shoved harder, confused as to what it could possibly be hung up on. It's just a board that rests in place…there should be nothing holding it down. It started to move but had – as he described – about thirty pounds of…something…on it. As the board began to tip, toys started falling all around him and he yelled, "Barb! You have to see this! What the f***?!"

I stared as colorful little things toppled down the ladder rungs, then I ran to get a flashlight. I went up the ladder and found some of the tubs had been opened and moved, and some toys had been taken out and left in little piles here and there. It had been one of the tubs that had been partially slid across the hatch.

My husband had been the ultimate skeptic until that night. He took the flashlight from me and went back into the attic to search for a "natural" reason for what we had witnessed. He found none. There was no evidence of animals and no opening where any might have gotten in. Aside from that, no tubs had been dumped. They were moved and only a select few had been opened. No other person had been up there in years. He had to admit that the only explanation he could come up with was paranormal. Someone unseen had been playing with our children's toys.

It happened again a few years later. While I was out one evening in 2016, my husband pulled the ladder up from the basement and tried to open the attic hatch. The night before, we had heard a loud bang and the sound of things falling. I thought for a moment that I heard a dragging or sliding movement, like an office chair moving along the floor.

My phone started dinging as he rapidly texted and sent me pictures. The hatch had been partially held down once more, this time with a tub of books. He had to move the board away at an angle in order to climb up. He checked for any signs of animals and there were none. Who or what was in the attic…first to play with the toys and then moving the books around? I believe I may have the answer.

Years before, in late 1999, I was lying in bed nursing my son when I heard my oldest child (then about five years old) coming down the hallway to get me. I was tucking the baby into his bed when I heard my daughter scream. I ran to find out what happened. She told me that there had been a little boy in my bedroom doorway, about the size of her sister.

"It wasn't so bad, Mommy," she said, "Until he pointed at me!"

Throughout the years, this little boy would make his presence known in little ways. Many times, I would be changing my son's diaper and sense that someone, a child, had come into the room with us. It was enough that I'd look over my shoulder. I have notes jotted throughout my journal… in February 2002, near morning, I felt two small hands touch my leg. When I moved over to let my son climb into bed beside me, no one was there. My little boy was asleep in the other room. November 2004, it was late, and I was in the living room. I heard my son moving around in the bedroom, on his way out to find me. When he toddled out of the bedroom, I saw a smaller boy, in shadow, follow behind him. The second little guy ran toward the kitchen and was gone.

Things culminated in July 2008. It was the early morning, and I was sleeping. I woke to someone shaking and tapping my shoulder. I rolled over quickly, figuring my husband needed me for something and got the strong scent of baby powder in my face. It came with a sense of "goodbye." There had been no baby powder in my house for at least six or seven years. That was the last I noticed the little boy with us. I believe he might have been the one enjoying the toys in the attic. If it wasn't him, then who?

And ponder this experience… April 2018. I walked into the kitchen one night to clean up after dinner and wash the dishes. The kids were off doing their own things; the house was quiet. There was a pot on the stove and a bowl of veggies to be covered and put away.

As I rounded the corner, I approached the counter beside the refrigerator. I saw that the serving spoon in the bowl had been bent completely in half and was now wrapped around the edge of the bowl. No one had been in the kitchen.

I stood and stared.

As a paranormal investigator, you'd think I'd react differently from anyone else… run to get my equipment, take photos from every conceivable angle, set up my voice recorders to see if I could get any EVPs. What did I do? I slid the spoon up and off the bowl, bent it back, and cleaned the kitchen. It's different when it happens in your own home. At least it is for me.

## In the Company of Angels

This one has been a true eye-opener for me and numerous other people. It started after I broke up with my boyfriend. My child and I moved back into my parents' house. It's an old farmhouse that's been converted to an apartment building. We had the top floor. My parents and siblings had the bottom. My daughter was around five years old at the time and started having what I thought were terrible nightmares. They became so terrible that she'd wake up crying, screaming and grasping, struggling to breathe and she soiled her pants. I felt bad for her and moved her into my room, hoping to soothe her nightmare issues and I bought a nightlight to hopefully help her feel secure.

One night, I woke up because I heard her starting to whine and cry. As I lifted my head and looked at her, I noticed a tall, lean shadow bending over my child. He looked to be dressed in what I call "Al Capone style" clothes. My first reaction was to yell, "What are you doing?! Get away from her!" It straightened up and vanished.

The figure was darker than anything I could see in the room. After that, I talked to multiple people, trying to find a way to keep my daughter safe. A nun that I'd made friends with gave me a cross blessed by the Pope. A Wiccan friend gave me a bell bracelet and a sage bundle. Another lady talked about putting the Bible under her pillow and a circle of salt around her bed…and so many more ideas. They all worked for a short period of time, then we'd move on to the next idea to try to get relief again. I was getting desperate as a mom watching her child be tormented. But, as time went on, the shadow man became more brazen. He would appear to adults and do a lot of different things, scaring people so badly we couldn't get anybody to stay past when the sun started to set.

My daughter started talking about a friend coming to help her, but I couldn't understand the name. I thought she was saying Megatron from the Transformers series, so I went with it. Whatever brought her comfort, I'd roll with. Anyway, one night, things became really bad. My sister (twenty-five years old), my brother (twenty years old), and I were sitting up, huddled around my daughter in the first-floor apartment, by a big bay window. We all had chills and the shadow man was throwing one heck of a tantrum, throwing things, knocking pictures off the wall and more. All of a sudden, my kid sighed, smiled, and said what sounded like, "Megatron is coming now. It will be okay." We all smiled and soothed her.

About that time, what felt like a sonic boom hit the house, knocking everything off the walls, rattling dishes in the cabinet, as a bright light-flash shined in from the deck outside the bay window. We could feel the difference in the atmosphere. All tension, fear and anger vanished. We were filled with peace. I covered my eyes and grabbed my kid tighter, and she hugged me as she giggled. My brother and sister gasped and whisper-screamed, "What was that?!"

As I picked up my head, I caught a glimpse of something white move past the bay window. My brother and sister turned to me asking if I saw it. I said, "Just a quick flash," and they both became fired up and they swore it was a big, white wing. My brother and I've always been the more curious and, apparently, stupid ones. I handed my daughter to my sister as I stood up with my brother and we headed outside to investigate.

When we came around the turn, it was a bright night that lit up the scenery amazingly. As we crossed the deck, we found a single white feather resting right in front of the bay window. We went back in and gave the feather to my daughter, who tucked it away in a box by her bed. We talked for a good while until the exhaustion hit us and we all went to bed.

As days went by, we all tried to find an explanation for what exactly happened. I took the feather to a wildlife expert that rehabs wildlife to see if they could tell me what the feather was from. After they had it for a few, they finally returned it and informed me that it was a dove feather. As I tried to process all of this and find reasons for it, my kid and I got talking more. She was getting frustrated because I kept asking her about Megatron. She told me that I was saying the name wrong. So, I got this random whim to search for names of angels because, after all, who else would have a white dove feather?

I about fell off my chair at the computer when I discovered the name of an angel listed. Metatron. He's a guardian of children. I still get chills to this day when I think of this experience. I've never heard of any angels except for the main ones mentioned in the King James version and the NIV Bible and such: Gabriel, Michael, Raphael, so I was truly mind-blown to find out about Metatron. He's mentioned in the Aggadah and in the mystical Kabbalistic texts with the rabbinic literature.

Anyway, now that I gave myself some serious goosebumps, I'm going to end this. Hopefully sharing these experiences will help bring some other people some closure. – *Shannon L.*

## Freakishly Tall…Without a Face!

My friends and I were at a desert party on the side of a mountain that has been long rumored to be haunted and cursed. It was about 3:30 a.m. and we decided to leave to go get breakfast at

Denny's as the party was pretty much over. Four girls piled into my car and four got into the other car. I led us out as I knew the roads well. We finally got onto the main (real) road; the other girls followed closely behind us. I thought I saw legs in the darkness ahead of us!

As my headlights hit the figure, I saw an extremely freakishly tall man. He had on jeans and a red and black flannel...but once the light hit his face, I froze in horror as he didn't really have a face! My foot let up off the pedal and my friends started screaming, "What the hell is that?! Go! Go! Go Niki, go!" He then raised his arms up and out and I swear his mouth stretched in an inhuman way as he started yelling and coming right at us! My friend in the front next to me pushed my leg down to push the gas, which made me snap out of it and drive out of there.

As we sped past him, he hit the back end of my car and went between my car and the girls behind us! We sped away, not stopping for stop signs or anything. Once we got to a well-lit parking lot, we parked and got out. Everyone in my car was freaking out about what had happened. Who or what was that?!

The other car pulled up asking, "What are you doing here?"

"What? You didn't see that guy try to attack us back there?"

They all said, "Huh? What guy? There was not a guy!" All four girls swore they saw nobody!

So, who or what did the four of us see come at the car? Why did the other car not see him? The only conclusion we all came to was that he was a ghost...I mean, think about it. It's 3:30 in the morning and he is walking toward the desert with no lights and had no definitive face. Maybe the urban legends of the area being haunted are true! – *Nicole G., Arizona*

## Is That You, Mom?

One day my daughter was walking up to our house and saw me in the window. She waved at me, and I smiled and waved back.

The door was locked, and she knocked and knocked, not understanding why I wasn't letting her in. So, she broke into the house through the back. Then, she saw the Post It note on the TV telling her I was at the store! – *Tamara, California*

## The Rising Mist

I never really had anything too crazy happen with my Ouija board; I would get normal communication. But a friend of mine had an old wooden one she had been given by her grandmother and that board we had a small experience with. When I tell the story, nobody believes me because it seems so farfetched.

There is this old building on Front Street that is presently used as a haunt in October, but when I was a teenager, it was just an abandoned building. We would often play hide and seek there. As far as the Ouija board experience, my friend and I decided to take her board in and try to contact whatever we believed was in the building.

**Side note: I also presently have a local paranormal team and we've researched and investigated the building and have found there are two confirmed deaths. It was also used to house Italian POWs. I didn't know then that the room we took the board into had been the room where they died. **

We began "playing" with the board and something started coming through. The responses were quick and short, the energy in the room felt thick and I remember it kind of felt hard to breathe. Almost a panicky feeling.

We were stupid young girls and asked basic questions:
"Do you need help?"
"Is there a light?"
"Are you nice?"
The planchette kept quickly moving to "No." Suddenly the planchette began to kind of vibrate and "float" ever so slightly above the board. We removed our fingers when it kept moving to "No," so, at this point, the movement was solely from an unseen force. Then,

from the middle of the board, a sort of purplish smoke began to rise. We screamed. She grabbed the board and we bolted. She tripped running down the stairs to the window we had crawled through and injured her hand pretty badly. I blame the spirit that was causing the events.

I'm pretty sure my friend kept the board, considering her grandmother gave it to her, but the last I knew (and this was almost twenty years ago), her parents had it locked in a box, in a locked storage unit. I wish I still spoke to her to find out if they had other experiences that caused them to lock it away, or if it was because of what happened to us. – *Kristin D., Colorado*

## Text 1 to Reply

It was August 2015. I had moved into my sister's house and my brother let me stay in his room while he went to his job…

That night, I was tossing and turning. The room felt heavy and intensely dark. I saw this peculiar red dot; I thought it was the clock. Turned it on, turned it off, and the red dots (two) were not in the same place where the alarm would be.

I felt like I hadn't slept, but it was five in the morning when I reached for my phone to scroll through the interwebs, I noticed a text message from a five/six-digit number that read, "Okay, that's my bed. Text '1' to reply or text '2' to unsubscribe and stop receiving messages" (something of that nature). My heart was pounding. I was sweating and pressed the two. It said, "Cannot respond. Unknown number."

But what the f***!! I was sooo scared I ran to my sister's room and let her read it. I took a screenshot of the text, but my phone had been acting up for the last week and I ended up deleting the text and screenshot.

It was wild. And scary. But mostly scary. AND IT'S TRUE! – *Linda N., Alabama*

## Lesson Learned

I was at a location, dummy me brings an object home. Had the worst week of bad luck, depression, cold energy. As soon as I got that object out of my home, that dark energy was gone. – *Tracy A., New York*

## Just Like Me

When I was growing up, my family lived in Reno, Nevada. I was four years old when my parents took my sisters and me to a cemetery in Virginia City. The day we arrived home, as my older sister and I were walking through the front door, we both fell flat on our faces as if something tripped us. Since that day our house became haunted, and we moved to Oregon a year after the occurrences first started.

At the time, my sisters and I – all three of us – shared a bedroom. I remember us always being afraid, especially at night. During the night is when my older sister, Jeni (she was five), and I would hear a female voice call out her name. It would repeat her name over and over again. "Jenifer...Jenifer..." We were terrified. My little sister was only two, so she doesn't remember any of this. On more than one occasion, I would wake up and feel as if something was watching me. I was always scared.

My mom had also experienced this presence and we all believed her to be a little girl about my age. My mom heard this little girl call out to her on numerous occasions and even saw her running down our hallway. My mother thought it was me because she said the little girl was wearing a nightgown similar to mine and had long blonde hair just like me. Mom said that when she saw the girl run down the hallway, she yelled at me, saying, "Danielle Nicole, stop running!" And it was only then that she looked over and saw that I was asleep on the couch. I actually remember this event as I remember waking up on the couch to my mom yelling at me.

The scariest incident was one night when my sisters and I were playing in our bedroom. It was dark outside, so we had the bedroom light on. Our parents were outside on the porch and as my sisters and I were playing, we heard something, or someone, run up and down the hallway. It was so vividly clear and so loud that we thought maybe our parents had come back inside. It wasn't them! These fast, loud footsteps were running back and forth down our hallway and straight toward our bedroom, which was directly at the end of the hall!

It got even scarier when we heard the running come toward us again and our bedroom light started flashing on and off. It flicked off then on, rapidly, twice in a row. We ran outside to our parents, screaming. They didn't believe us and told us to go back inside. We did as we were told and no sooner than five minutes later, upon playing in our room, we heard the running footsteps come down the hall and, once again, our light started flicking on and off. We ran outside a second time and finally our parents let us stay outside until it was time for bed.

We were terrified. We always believed that this little girl followed us home from the cemetery that day in Virginia City, but of course, we don't know for certain. What I do know is that there was more than one presence in that house as the female voice calling my sister's name was NOT a little girl. On top of that, my mom, older sister and myself had seen three shadow figures on separate occasions. Each time we saw them, all three were together and appeared to be walking toward us. It looked like a man and two children because of their size. I'm not sure who they could've been, but they terrified us and they would not go away until, whichever one of us was seeing them would say, "The Lord is my Shepard," three times in a row.

I never did find out who the female could have been as we never saw a female figure other than the little girl. All I know for sure is that ever since, in every house I have lived in, there has been a little girl presence. The same girl? Perhaps. Perhaps I'm just sensitive to these things and maybe they're all different spirits. I can't say for sure.

I have dreams quite often about a little girl who looks exactly like me except her hair is darker and she always has a sinister aura about her. It's utterly terrifying. Sometimes she's my age now, sometimes she's younger and sometimes she's older than me. My little sister swears she's even seen this girl I dream about in real life on more than one occasion and says it scares her, too. She has seen her around ever since I was eight years old, which would make my sister six at the time, and she always thinks it's me until she calls out my name. She said every time she does, thinking this girl is me, the girl looks at her with an evil type of grin and then she's gone. What's really interesting to me is that I was eight years old when I started dreaming about this girl who looks like me but isn't me. She terrifies me even to this day, and yes, I still dream of her. – *Danielle S., Oregon*

## Heartbreak Foretold

Back in 1968, when I was nine years old, I received a Ouija board for Christmas. My neighborhood friend, Patty, and I decided to play with it in my basement. One of the questions we asked was, "Who would die first in our families?" It said our mothers. In between Christmas 1968 and January 4th, 1969, my mom had gone into the hospital for a scheduled surgery. On January 4th (the day after my birthday), my mom died from a blood clot to her lungs. She was only fifty-one years old.

I never touched that Ouija board again and never told my family what happened. I recently caught up with Patty through Facebook. We haven't kept in touch since high school. The Ouija board prediction did not hold true for her. She told me her father died first in her family.

Back in 1968 we did not know what we know now about Ouija boards. Besides, we were only nine years old back then. I have learned through the years that Ouija boards are something to stay away from. You're only asking for trouble. – *Tiffany R., Florida*

## A Red Apparition

My ex-husband and I lived in a haunted trailer. The baby swing would take off with our son not even in it. The heat would come on by itself in the dead of summer. The back door opened on its own. Our last straw was when we saw something unexplainable in our bedroom one night. There was a red apparition beside our bed. It scared my ex-husband and me so bad. I remember saying to him that night, "What is that?"

He said, "I don't know, but we're getting out of here."

We got our baby boy and got out of there. Our car didn't want to start, but it finally did. We left that night and only went back to pack up and move. We found creepy drawings in there. From the first night we moved in, when I was pregnant, the energy was bad. I would lay there and cry. I hated it. You would hear people talking when you were there by yourself. It was crazy!!! – *Jana W.*

## But Was It a Cat?

Most notable for me was when I was in my twenties and moved into an older house. I learned that a girl had committed suicide there many years prior. The most memorable thing was the constant feeling of dread and being watched. But there were physical anomalies as well...such as beer bottles falling over or falling off tables as if they had been pushed. There were also temperature shifts where spots in the house were quite cold while others were hot.

But . . .

The most unusual thing was the giant black cat you could only see out of the corner of your eye. It would appear in a back stairwell and vanish without a sound when you looked at it head-on. Other occupants had seen the cat as well and experienced the same phenomena as me. – *Nathan B., Kentucky*

## Haunted Decatur, Illinois

Approximately seventeen years ago, during a late September day, I mentioned going on a short trip to Decatur. My husband, Mario, our teenage daughter, Audrey, and her friend, Jessie, accompanied me on a visit to one of the most haunted towns in the nation.

We arrived at the Greenwood Cemetery around 2:00 in the afternoon. It was an overcast day and there was no one there but the four of us. The numerous oak trees with huge trunks and the very worn tombstones made us immediately realize that this cemetery was quite old. It existed during the Civil War and many soldiers from both the North and the South are buried there. As we made our way to that area, we could see four or five rusted cannons. We had read that due to a nearby train route, many soldiers arrived in Decatur. The Southern soldiers were prisoners, and many were injured during battle. As they lay dying, mass graves were dug. In a hurry to rid themselves of the soon-to-be smelly corpses, the Northern soldiers flung them like discarded sacks of potatoes into these mass graves. Often, the injured were not yet dead and were consequently buried alive. Their tormented souls remain in that cemetery where they took their last breaths.

We came upon the small set of stairs where some have witnessed the apparition of "a weeping woman."

I sat on those steps and Audrey took a picture of me. After inspecting that picture, we found that I had this horrid, crazed look on my face as my eyes seemed to bulge from their sockets. A truly hair-raising sight!

Jessie was going to sit in an old stone chair by a nearby grave, but I cautioned her not to as it was very ominous looking. Although it was made of cement, it had been fashioned into pieces of large, twisted branches. It gave me the creeps.

We walked into the shadow cast by a large fifteen-foot cross made of heavy metal which had since rusted over. It would have been dazzling in its day but now it stood as a sorrowful, weathered and steadfast sentinel, an omen of this cemetery. Audrey posed in front of it, and I snapped two pictures. When later looking at these pictures (that we downloaded on our home computer), we saw that one was perfect while the other was fuzzy from the ground up to Audrey's waist. It's as if there were some sort of magnetic force/energy being given off.

Around a curve lay a grave to the right of us. It had been tampered with years earlier by mischievous teens and was said to be haunted. We felt an eerie vibe being near it. Heading back toward the car, a strong wind started up where there had been absolute calm. The leaves on the massive oak trees rattled as the wind shook their branches and they waved wildly as if beckoning to us. The sky darkened and hundreds of crows flew overhead. Their black bodies descended upon the cemetery like torpedoes into the oak trees! Their crazily flapping wings and loud caws made us flee in fear to the car as they darted about us. It was like a scene out of the movie, "The Birds," by Alfred Hitchcock!

We needed no further coaxing to vacate the premises. Upon arriving in the downtown area of Decatur, we walked to the Ford Theater. Its employees said they had experienced numerous ghostly apparitions. The doors were locked as we attempted to enter the building, so I took a picture of Audrey and Jessie standing in front of its huge glass doors. When we looked at that picture, we could all clearly see the distinct image of a woman wearing a bonnet and a long dress who was standing directly behind them!! That knocked our socks off with fright! We all pointed at that image on the computer screen, screaming in disbelief.

I had taken various pictures of downtown buildings, most of which later revealed that same fuzzy magnetic field from the ground up to maybe two feet (other pictures taken after our Decatur visit had no such fuzziness and were quite perfect).

We went into one of the quaint little shops located around the plaza and abruptly stopped in our tracks as we spotted a bona fide "witch" man. He was very unusual looking besides being totally dressed in black and wearing a black top hat to match. His face was unforgettable because it didn't seem real. Yet, it was. He walked looking downwards the whole while, totally determined to get to wherever he was going. We planned to venture toward the river, but it was getting dark, so we decided to head home. – *Vicki K.L.W.*

**Note: *Pictures of Greenwood Cemetery are on the Decatur Illinois website where you can see the contorted cement "branch" chair we saw as well as cannons, the tall cross, the short steps, the huge oak trees, and the cemetery itself. There are also pictures of the haunted downtown theater.*

## Poke the Eyeball

I met my fiancé on a dating website and decided to move in with him. A week went by. I had my makeup bag on the bathroom sink while I was in the tub getting a bath and washing my hair. All of a sudden, I watched my makeup bag fly off the sink, almost like someone smacked it off. I was scared and jumped out of that bathroom, naked, to my bedroom. It got worse, though.

I brought my two-year-old daughter to live with us. She kept talking to someone not there physically and poking at a hole in the wall. She was saying, "Both men," but what we finally got out of her was, "Poke the eyeball." I was a little weirded out and my boyfriend looked at me and said his girls had seen an eyeball in that same wall, same hole, years before we got there. He had plastered it and didn't notice a hole again until my daughter said that. I was totally freaked out!!! Knowing his girls had seen it years ago, and my daughter saying that, creeped me out! – *Christina M., Pennsylvania*

## Ghosts and Spirits in My House

The first spirit I saw was my aunt a year after she died. Not long afterward, my sister messed with a spirit board and others showed up, some of them dark. One of the light spirits walked the halls of my house until she got in bed with my dad for some "fun." The dark one messed with my sister until she moved out and then came after me. It took a long time to get it away from me. Dark shadow people are still seen in my house by others, but they don't mess with me anymore. *James J.*

## Double Take

I moved into my daughter's home about two years ago. My granddaughters had been telling me of paranormal experiences they were having before I moved in. Nothing horrible, just weird.

One evening, while watching TV with my youngest grandchild, I noticed down the hall I could see the patio doors and the reflection of the room behind them. I noticed that my other granddaughter was dancing in front of the doors. She was wearing shorts and her hair was up in a bandana. As she danced back and forth, I would lose sight of her for a second and then see her dance again.

I mentioned to my youngest granddaughter that her sister must be feeling chipper because she was dancing. My youngest granddaughter went to see what her sister was doing and, lo and behold, she was sitting on her bed, reading, dressed in a hoodie and sweats and she had her lights dimmed. There's no way she could've changed that fast. She didn't know what I was talking about when I told her what I saw.

I know what I saw! I also know it wasn't my granddaughter. It must've been her doppelgänger. The only thing odd that I did notice was that her reflection made her legs look really skinny and I just thought it was the reflection in the glass that did that. – *Deborah F., Idaho*

## Something's Watching

This happened in Nebraska. When I was little, I shared a room with my sister. One night I got really thirsty and went downstairs to ask my mom for a drink of water. While she was getting me a drink, we heard a loud scream come from my bedroom that sounded like my sister. My mom and I ran upstairs, and I heard momma asking my sister what was wrong.

"Momma, make them stop staring at me!"

"Who? Who is staring at you, baby?" Momma asked.

"The eyes, Momma, the eyes!" and when my momma looked where my sister was pointing, she saw the eyes on the wall across from my sister's bed! As soon as my momma started praying, the eyes disappeared! – *Melanie M.*

## Lottery Numbers, Please

This is going to sound really strange to some people but, believe it or not, Ouija boards are not bad or evil. Yes, it is true that we do not really know who we are calling forward but when we do know, the results can be AMAZING, as you are about to read.

I was on an investigation at Coalhouse Fort which is at Tilbury in Essex, England. The investigation took a bit of a turn when I got caught up in a spiritual love triangle so what happened when we started the Ouija board session was of great joy. More on that later.

The board was set up in the middle of a room and we all stood around it. It was quite a large board, and we were using a glass as the planchette. We were instructed to place the tips of our fingers on the top of the glass. There were quite a few of us so there was plenty of energy in the room for the spirits to use to communicate, if needed.

We began. At first, as is usual, the glass did not move. Then, after a few minutes, we noticed some slight movement and asked if the spirit had a message for anyone in the room. The glass shifted toward Sue and gave us her initials. Sue is a member of my team, Essex Ghost Investigations, and it was her nan coming through.

As we proceeded to ask questions, the glass was all over the board and I felt the spirit of her nan was disoriented. I asked her if this was the case and the glass moved to YES. In my mind's eye, I saw how she passed and asked, "Are you showing me how you passed?"

YES. Her nan confirmed it. It felt to me as if Sue never really had a clear answer about her nan's passing and this was her nan's opportunity to let her know.

After Sue's nan gave us this message, the glass stopped moving for about a minute or so. Her nan had left. When the glass moved again, I asked if this was a different spirit and the glass slid to YES. Now, we had to work out who this one was and why the spirit was there.

People worry about if they will take spirits home with them and my answer to that has been if you take any spirits home with you, it is more likely you brought them with you in the first place. I didn't know how close to home this spirit would be until a few key points came up which only myself, and my nephew Danny, knew and could confirm. Danny is also a member of my team.

When we asked who this spirit had a message for, the glass moved toward Danny. I asked if the spirit was related to Danny.

NO.

I asked if the spirit was related to me.

YES.

To my dad?

YES.

So, I said, "You are related to me and my dad but not Danny. Is that correct?"

YES.

Now at this point I asked if the spirit knew any other members of my family and the spirit spelled out the names of my sister and Danny's brother. Danny and I looked at each other because, like I said at the start, it was only Danny and myself who knew this information out of everyone in the room and I was the only one who knew about the connection between the spirit, myself and my dad but not to Danny.

I then asked the spirit if it was there when Danny passed away for a few moments on the operating table.

YES.

"Were you the one that brought Danny back to us?"

Once more the glass moved to YES.

By this time, I was pretty certain that I knew who it was, so I thanked the spirit for looking after Danny and bringing him back to us. Although I was fairly sure of who the spirit could be, I asked for either some initials or a name.

The spirit slid the glass over to the letters W... G... C.

It confirmed to me who it was. My Grandad Cook. While alive, he always had a great sense of humour, so I thought to myself, let's see if he still does.

There is one question I get asked a lot when I tell people I am a medium and that is, "Do you know the lottery numbers?" or "Have you ever asked the ghosts for the lottery numbers?" Well, on this day, I went one better. I actually asked for the lottery numbers while on the Ouija board! So, I can now honestly answer, "Yes, I have asked for the lottery numbers," when people ask.

When I asked, the glass moved to the zero. Everyone got

excited and couldn't believe not only did the spirit know but was going to go along with it. We had someone with us who was part of running the event and they had a pen and pad, so I said, "Right, get ready to write these numbers down."

I asked for the first number and the glass moved to five and then returned to zero.

I didn't know if it was five or fifty because I don't play the lottery and it had recently changed its format with more numbers. After this the glass moved to six and back to zero, seven and to zero.

By this time, I could see what was going on. The glass moved to eight and back to zero. I asked, "Spirit, are you having a laugh with us?"

YES.

"Go on then, you might as well finish it off!" Sure enough, the glass moved to the nine and then back to zero.

I said, "Yeah, thanks spirit," and laughed. How could you not after something like that? To me it felt as if I had taken my grandad with me, and he used that time to finally say hello and have some fun. My grandad gave information that would be the quickest way to confirm who it was and that only led to better things.

So, can Ouija boards be dangerous? Yes, they can but they are only as dangerous as the intentions of the people who use them. Just like any other piece of equipment, really. Use them in a sensible and respectful manner and it can be a great communication tool. I have NEVER had any bad experiences on a Ouija board.

The first time I ever used a Ouija board was at Eastbury Manor House. I had a spirit affect me as soon as I walked into the room. I stood there and did not say a word. I must have been standing there for a good few minutes before I put down the cameras I was holding, turned around and walked out of the room.

While I was out there, the group leader and my friend's mum came out to check on me and, just as I got myself together to go back into the room, I went down on one knee and started crying. Shortly after, I managed to get myself into the room and there were three people sitting at the Ouija board ready to start the session.

I said to my teammate Brian, "Do you want to go on the board, and I'll do the filming?"

"Yeah, okay."

I thought that would be better because of the way the spirit affected me. The group leader told the people at the board to place the tips of their fingers on the glass and, when they did, he started asking the questions.

At first, like I mentioned at the start of this, the glass did not move. The group leader asked everyone to remove their fingers and place them back on. He once again asked questions and, once again, the glass did not move. He couldn't understand why the glass wasn't moving and not long after he joined the others on the Ouija board. He continued asking questions with no responses on the board, no movement at all. Not even one millimeter.

I had an idea and I said to Brian, "Get up and let me try, seeing as how it affected me."

Brian and I swapped places and I put the tip of my finger on the glass. The group leader, still baffled, asked questions once again. Nothing.

I thought since it affected me, let's see what happens if I ask a question. "Is the spirit that affected me here with us now?" To everyone's surprise, the glass moved to YES. The spirit had chosen me to communicate with because it only responded to my voice. I could tell it was not bad or dangerous and I didn't feel threatened at all.

When I asked for the spirit's name, the glass moved to all different letters so I don't believe the spirit could see clearly enough to give us the letters we needed to make out who it was. The spirit did feel sad and depressed, and wanted answers to some things that had happened to him and the woman he was in love with. I managed to give him that the next time I was there.

You see, the spirit's fiancée hung herself due to being raped and abused by the dignitary staying there and had ended up pregnant.

This would have caused a lot of disgrace and dishonour to both families and, since she couldn't deal with the shame, she, sadly, ended her own life.

Now you may think that this could be classed as a bad experience, but I see it as a good one because I was able to help a spirit get the answers he needed. He could now rest and know he had been loved by his fiancée. I would not have been able to do this without going on the Ouija board after I was affected by the spirit's emotions. – *David Cook, Essex Ghost Investigations. David is also the host of The Ghostly Hour on kcorradio.com.*

## Games with a Ghost

This is one of my favorite experiences at this particular home. I've lived in several haunted houses over the years. This one was in Frenchville, Maine, way up at the northernmost tip of the state, right on the St. John River. The house was built in 1849, which made it older than the town itself. At some point over the years, it was converted into a duplex. When we bought it, my husband and I lived in one side, my mom in the other. Our side of the house was always a little creepy to say the least. A little side note: The area where we live is very, very French. We speak it still to this day.

My hubby (now ex, but that's a whole other horror story), his uncle Mike, cousin Sara and I were hanging out, playing our new Xbox Kinnect. It was my turn, and I was playing the dodgeball game that comes with the thing. Out of nowhere, there was another person on the screen with me. A little girl, pigtails and all, playing the game. We were a little freaked out, so I sat down, we smoked a joint, and the game went to the resting screen, where the character stands waiting, tapping its foot, scratching its head and looking around.

We sat there for a little while when the character woke up, shook itself and started moving around. There was no one in front of the camera. We were all sitting on the sectional sofa. I started explaining how to play the game: take your hand and put it on the arrow and swipe it to the left. She was getting the right motion but not in the right place.

I told my ex to tell her in French. AND SHE FREAKING PUT HER HAND ON THE ARROW AND PROCEEDED TO PLAY THE DAMN GAME. She did pretty well! He talked her through it, in French.

We tried to recreate the whole thing. I stood there playing the game and Sara stood on her knees next to me to see if the camera would pick up two people when it was only set for one player. It wouldn't pick up a second player!

The house was torn down last winter. I drove by when it was almost gone, and I had to pull over and cry. It was a sad house. It always felt really heavy, especially the side we lived in. There were a million times I saw someone walk by on the porch when no one was out there. A lady died there several years before we moved in, on the porch roof where those two wires come in from the road. She was painting and hit the wires and was electrocuted.

The original owner/builder died there in 1870-something. The little girl spirit, though... A friend of mine went over with me to clean it out several years after I moved. She is psychic and said the girl child was hiding under the house, hiding from "him," the man with the big heavy boots that would pace the floor above her. She had a place to hide in the corner of the crawlspace.

We went down to the basement to see the crawlspace. There's an area in the front corner that looked like it was dug out...impossible to reach for a normal sized adult.

At night we would be in bed and hear someone walking around downstairs. It drove the dog nuts. I never got a name for the little girl, but my friend said that she sent her home, toward the light. I only hope she made it there and isn't hanging around an empty lot. Poor thing! – *Jessica D., Maine*

# Leave it Alone

When I was a teen, my friends and I played around with a Ouija board for a while. I always figured my friends were pushing it, but then one day the planchette started moving around like crazy. It went really fast and stopped at letters too quickly for us to even follow what was being spelled. It went so incredibly fast that none of my friends could have been doing it and we were scared. We quit and never touched it again. – *Lucille H., New York*

# The Science Project

When I attended St. Ignatius Elementary School, I never really had faith that God existed or if I believed in anything. Sure, I said all my prayers and went to church and did everything that the priests and nuns told me to do, but I never really had any awareness of God, angels, devils, etc. I have had paranormal experiences at the house I lived in, but even then, I wasn't sure if what I experienced was real or in my head.

Every year the school would host a science project fair. My two friends and I would pick a subject, do the research, and make a poster board. Each year it was something different and, for reasons not remembered, that year we chose to do our science project on Satan. Maybe we thought it was cool or weird, but I was totally into it. I was curious because I didn't know anything about the devil except what the church told us, and I wanted to see for myself what the hype was all about.

We went to the library and proceeded to look for every book we could find on Satan. We had a nice big stack, and I was excited to read up on this mysterious character I was taught to despise. When we went to check out, the librarian was shocked and looked scared. Here we were, young Catholic girls in our uniforms taking out books that seemed contradictory to our innocent faces. She gave us a warning and asked if we really wanted the books. She said we didn't know what we were getting ourselves into. We laughed and said we weren't worried about it.

When we left the library, I couldn't carry everything so one of my friends said that she would take most of the books because she was getting a ride home. I told her I could take a couple of the books because I had to walk home, and our other friend said that she couldn't take any books home because her parents would be very upset if they saw the subject.

When I got home, I started reading and I didn't know what the fuss was about. I wasn't scared at all and, actually, it was very interesting because I learned so much that I hadn't known before. I guess it was a morbid curiosity. Or maybe rebelliousness since I knew my parents wouldn't approve.

In the early evening, I received a phone call from the friend who took most of the books home. She was screaming on the phone that her older brother shot himself in the head in front of his friends and entire family. At first, I thought she was joking but she was hysterical. When I realized it was true, I felt a cold chill start from the top of my head, all the way down my body to my feet, and then a stabbing pain in my stomach like I was pierced with a knife. I came down with a fever and was nauseated instantaneously. Her brother had been an expert with firearms and knew all the safety precautions. There was no reason why he would put a gun to his head and shoot himself in front of his family and friends. I later heard from different people that he thought the gun was empty and was playing around when he did this horrible thing, and he had a smile on his face the entire time.

That entire week I was in bed with the flu and missed school. I found out the funeral was going to be held at the church and some instinct inside of me knew I had to attend the service. My parents told me I couldn't go because I was sick, but I insisted I had to be there. I begged and begged and finally my father agreed to take me, but I had to sit in the back of the church in case I had to throw up again. I walked into the church hunched over in pain and sat in the very last pew. I was weak and feeling terrible, but I knew I had to be there for my best friend. The stabbing pains were still there but my stubbornness to be in church was more powerful.

When the priest holding the thurible made his way down the aisle, with the altar boy carrying a giant cross, and reached where I was sitting, I smelled the santo palo incense and immediately felt better. It was as if I had never been sick at all. It was in that moment I knew God and the devil were real. All of my experiences since then have given me a sense of comfort knowing that I am not imagining things and that in this world there are things unknown and yet to be identified, experienced, and explored. We never did that stupid science project, and we returned all the books without telling anyone what had happened. – *Lena C., California*

## It Licked My Hand

I've had several paranormal experiences but the one that sticks with me and was the scariest thing I've encountered happened over the course of a few days...maybe even weeks...I'm not sure, honestly, but I know it happened close together.

I have always been the type to "feel" things. When I was about fifteen years old, my mom and I, and my dog Bon Bon, lived in a little white house. One night I was in the living room straightening my hair and doing my makeup in a big mirror I had set up. From the mirror you could see the hallway behind me. I kept feeling someone staring and it wasn't a good feeling. It happened a few times and I got so scared I went beside my entertainment center so whatever it was couldn't see me. I pretty much prayed for it to go away.

I felt the presence again and my little rat terrier (who was not aggressive at all) got up on the edge of the couch and started growling and snarling at something invisible to the human eye.

Yet another night, I was up late watching TV in the living room, and I heard my mom's door open. I muted the TV thinking I was about to be in trouble. I looked up and saw a strange, distorted version of my mom. Its head was turned away from me and it walked with a creepy movement, almost robotic/zombie-ish? It went into the dark hallway and disappeared. I thought it was my mom going to the bathroom and I was going to scare her when she got back, so I went into her room to wait. My mom was asleep in bed! I jumped into the bed with her!

Another time, I saw three cone-head shadows walking (more like bobbing up and down and going back and forth) past my window. Now this was strange because my window set up high and we had a screened-in back porch that my window was in.

Another night I got in bed and, for some reason, hung my hand over the edge (which I NEVER do because someone could grab your hand like in scary movies...). I immediately thought, "Why did I do that?" and something licked my hand!! I tried to rationalize and thought, "Oh, that's Bon Bon," but felt with my feet that Bon Bon was under the blanket and had been there the whole time.

I felt something in my face with pure hatred, disgust and I could tell it wanted me dead. It wanted to take my light is the best way I can explain it. I clenched my eyes extremely tight and started praying (in my head, not out loud) for protection.

"Please protect me, please protect me, please protect me." Over and over and over.

Though my eyes were closed, I saw a bright light enter my room and, immediately, peace came over me.

Whatever it was had gone and has NEVER returned!! Since then, I've kind of tried to block out things that I see or feel. I don't give them attention or fear. I always try to rationalize what I see or debunk it. But, sometimes, they are persistent and make themselves known. I've learned from this that I am protected, and something out there saved me from that thing. Some say it's God. Others have said it was my own power/faith... Whatever it was, I'm thankful. – *Maddison H., Arkansas*

6

*WHEN SOMETHING UNSEEN*
*REVELS IN PLAYING TRICKS WITH YOUR MIND,*
*FEEDS ON YOUR FEAR...*
*THAT'S WHEN EVERYTHING TAKES...*

# A DARKER TURN

While a lot of supposed paranormal activity can be debunked and the remaining attributed to spirits who once walked this earth, there is that small percentage of things that roam the shadows. Ghouls, demons and darker entities, existing on the fringe, waiting for an opportunity to wreak havoc on anyone they can.

In my nearly nine years of investigating, and forty-plus years of researching and living with the paranormal, I've been lucky enough to not run into anything truly evil. The team has met up with some grumpy spirits and those who were not aware they had passed, considering us intruders in "their" homes. We did a walkthrough before an investigation in a museum one night where a team member and I were stopped in our tracks. Housed in that room were the possessions of a woman who had once held a prominent position in the town. It had been as if we'd hit an invisible wall, and the feeling was one of, "This is my space." Of course, we were respectful and backed off.

The most concerning experience, though, happened recently and very close to home. My niece and her oldest son were visiting for the weekend, and they decided to explore a pull-off next to a small lake about two-tenths of a mile from my house. Her son is into nature, and they hiked, taking photographs along the way. A little farther up the road from where they parked their car, they noticed a set of stone steps leading up the bank across the road. They walked over to see where it led.

My niece watched as her son went up the steps, crossing the "threshold" and into a small clearing surrounded by an old, stone foundation. He had his metal detector in hand and was heading toward a stream where he saw something shining. His mother approached the steps but stopped. She didn't want to continue as the entire area felt wrong, but her son had gone farther in, and she wasn't going to let him go on alone. She crossed into the clearing a foot or two before stopping again. She couldn't go further. They both felt they were being watched. Her son sensed that, whatever it was, was being drawn to the beeping of his detector, so he switched it off. On its final beep, it seemed to him that the "thing" watching them, which had been looking at his mother, slowly turned its head to glare at him. He described it to me later as the feeling of a hunter sizing up his prey.

They both looked in the direction of whatever was watching them, and confirmed whatever it was, was straight ahead. That was all it took, and my niece told her son they needed to get to the car...now. Urgency sent them moving.

As she drove, her son kept looking behind them. He felt that they were being followed and, when they returned to my house and entered the basement, he felt compelled to lock the door. This was not something he normally did, but he sensed it was necessary.

They walked up the stairs into my living room and immediately told us about their encounter. My niece said something had wanted them OUT. That they disturbed something, and it would go to any and all lengths to make sure they wouldn't do it again. Her son told me he has a great imagination and described what he thought the creature looked like. A tall, dark mass. Bright red eyes.

Long arms and big hands. Huge. It wasn't his imagination, in my opinion.

While he had been in the basement, he found a small selenite tower on the floor and set it next to the basement door. It had always resided on a shelf at the rear of the large room, and I don't know how it made its way to where he found it when he needed it.

After they told us about their experience, I went downstairs to check on my laundry and, as I stepped off my stairs onto the cold cement, I glanced at the door. My first reaction was, and I said it out loud, "No!" Also odd for me...but it felt like it needed to be said, as if I was setting a boundary. A "This is MY house, and you are NOT allowed inside" assertion. I asked my niece if she thought it would help her son if I saged the basement. She thought it would be a good idea. He joined me. When I was done, he paused and opened the basement door to see if the entity had gone. He stood for a few seconds, then shut the door again and locked it. He said the feeling had dissipated but that whatever it was, was still close.

I have driven by those steps and that foundation nearly every day for the last thirty-five years. They seem out of place, and I've been curious enough to wonder about them...and always believed I would check them out "sometime," but never stopped (it never occurred to me that that was unusual, but now, yes, as an investigator, how weird that I wasn't diving right into the site of an old, abandoned property, examining the foundation and area for clues, recording for EVP's, taking photos, etc.). Now, I will be researching what stood on that site in the past and what might have happened there.

A few interesting notes: My grandnephew mentioned that around the area, and on both sides of the stairway, there was garbage from people who had passed through...bottle caps, condoms and the like. There was no trash on the steps themselves. Also, when my niece and her son were leaving the next day, I received a text when they were a few miles away. As they were driving past that spot, my grandnephew was going to take a picture of the area. He said that the clearing was gone, and he didn't see the steps. I drove the road later in the day and I couldn't find the steps, either. That struck me as it would take an enormous amount of energy and intent to mask a clearing and stairway. Whatever this creature was, it was strong.

I was considering what this could possibly be and why it would be in that area, to decide on the best way to research the property. There had been a stone foundation and steps as long as I could remember, so whatever house had been there was long since gone when I first noticed the steps more than forty years ago. Why had no one lived in the home after the last owner? Why had it been left to disintegrate over time? What had drawn this "thing" there? Had it been present in the home or had some ritual been done on the site years later, as kids came and went, using the small clearing as a meeting place?

I contacted my friend and fellow investigator, David Cook. He is the host of The Ghostly Hour on kcorradio.com and is a medium. I gave him the details of the encounter and asked if he could sense anything or tell me more about what was going on at that site. The following is what he messaged me.

*Feels like it was an old man who lived out there for many years and felt like he was forgotten about, which he liked but also resented. He had enough of life in a town and just wanted to be left alone. He became bitter and angry at the world. True he was a hunter and fisherman for food. The image your niece's son saw was basically him trying to scare them away and it might have followed them a certain way to ensure they kept going and didn't turn around to go back.*

*There have been loads of reports of people taking certain routes then, when they went back the same way, things had changed. As long as they don't go back then neither of them should have anything to worry about.*

It took another day until I found the steps again. I drove

slowly along the road, searching the overgrown bank to catch sight of them. I repeated in my mind, "I don't want to disturb you and I won't go up the steps. I just want to see where they are so that I can avoid them." The steps that had been hidden since the encounter were visible once more.

My grandnephew mentioned the day after the experience that a few of his close friends had messaged him to see if he was okay. They said the day before felt off and they wanted to make sure everything was fine.

There are plenty of angry spirits in this world and are just that...angry. Not demonic. But when something can wield enough energy that can mask a clearing and plant images in your mind, it can absolutely do more. When something says, "Get out," you do.

**Update:** In the months following this incident, the spirit that had been residing at the site has attempted to communicate with members of my family and, in fact, followed my niece and her son to their home. He became quite loud in his demand to be heard but, once he had our attention, calmed down. He hadn't realized he didn't need to yell for someone to listen. What we've discerned is as follows:

We believe his name is John (last name S--). He was more than an angry spirit; he was in a rage for many decades. The only date we could get from him was 1783. I don't know the significance but if I had to guess, I'd say it was his death date. He was murdered. His wife was raped and murdered; their only child killed. Justice was at the forefront of his mind.

In addition to his hatred of those who carried out this violent act on his family, John was also heartbroken and upset as he stated his child had not been properly buried. He was searching for his family and couldn't find them.

During the course of our conversations with John, I had the Ovilus running. A few of the words it said during our sessions were:

Jon (its spelling)
Funeral (twice)
Shoulder
Discernment
Violent
Hobble
Forever
Indirect Voice
Crossover
Blind

At one point, John broke from trying to communicate about his situation and decided to "prove" to us that he was legitimate. He started giving information about someone with a hurt foot. As we tried to figure out, interpret, apply what he was saying to the people around us, he got more direct and specific with the information. It was the left foot, the big toe...and my niece said she felt he was laughing about it all. He went so far as to say it was an issue stemming from an ingrown toenail.

My jaw dropped. Not that I'm sure why it did, after all the investigations I've been on and the things I've experienced with spirits throughout my life, but it did. He was speaking about me. All day long, I'd had a toe that was quite sore...and it stemmed from issues with ingrown toenails I'd had when I was a child, to the point that I had surgery on that foot. I told my niece it was me (texted, actually, as we were in two different states as John "house hopped" between us). She said that he was then satisfied – that we knew he was real and on the level, and that we would figure this all out. He felt at peace.

One other thing John let us know was that the entity my niece and her son saw/felt that day in the clearing was not him. There is something else there. Something dark that was drawn to him and his negativity. Feeding off his rage and resentment. It is still there, and I believe it will stay until we can convince John that he can move on. Cross over. Find his family on the other side. But, until then, my team and I will not cross those steps. I continue to research the site and have enlisted the aid of the assessor's office, the county historian and another, trusted, psychic. We will try to find John his answers and help him move on.

## Stay Out of the Basement

One of my many experiences happened at my grandparents' home. My mother and I were helping my grandma shortly after my grandpa passed away. It was a mild summer day with the sun shining outside. My mother and I were in one of the attics, cleaning it out. This attic had no windows and only two hanging lights that were basically light bulbs hanging from wires with pull strings attached. One was at the entrance, and one was somewhat in the middle. The floor was old wood planks that weren't in very good shape but were sturdy.

We had been working about an hour when we started to hear some scraping noises toward the dark part of the attic, toward the front of the house. We saw nothing when we looked in that direction. I headed that way to grab some of the trash bags I had filled and began to feel uneasy. The hair on my arms stood on end and goosebumps developed. I stopped in my tracks. I heard the scraping noise again. I looked around, trying to see if I could see a squirrel or some other animal. Again, I saw nothing, so I grabbed a couple of bags and started to walk toward the other end of the attic where the narrow door to the hallway was located. I had just walked past the light in the middle when out of nowhere we heard someone running fast toward us in boots.

We glanced at each other, and I dropped the bags. We both exited the attic, slamming the door. We stood there with our hearts beating fast, trying to catch our breath. I looked at my mother and said, "Mom, ghosts can go through walls!" We ran down the stairs all the way to the living room where my grandmother was sitting in her chair. She looked at us and asked what happened. We told her and she said, simply, "I have been hearing more noises from that attic, such as scraping and hard footsteps and noises like bangs from the basement." My mother and I both knew Grandma was telling the truth. We left to go home shortly later, but that wasn't the end.

My grandparents' home was one of the first homes built on her street. It is said the original owner was a very controlling and possessive man who married a beautiful younger woman. She became pregnant and gave birth to a baby boy. The husband had no interest in the baby and was jealous because he took all of her attention. One day, the mom took a nap and, when she woke, the baby was not in his cradle. The woman searched for him and then heard noises coming from the basement. She opened the door and asked her husband if he knew where the baby was. He said he was playing with him. She became scared and walked down into the basement, asking where the baby was. The man pointed to the coal bucket by the coal furnace where he'd left the murdered child. The woman screamed so loudly the neighbors heard and the husband then shoved his wife into the coal furnace and burned her to death. The older couple who lived across the street told my grandparents the information shortly after they moved in.

Why did I include this information? A few days after the incident in the attic, we moved into my grandparents' home. After moving in, we would hear a baby crying in the area of the stairs that led to the upstairs and passed over the stairs that led to the basement. We would hear a woman scream or be crying in the same area.

One time, we were in the basement cleaning it out. I did not want to be down there. I had a bad feeling, like someone or something was watching me when I was in the left side of the basement. I say "left" because the stairs split the basement into two areas. One side had an open area with the gas furnace and hot water tank. My grandma had my grandpa replace the coal furnace after they moved in. The other side had a workspace and shelving with old jars full of food my grandma had canned years ago. I was on the left side bagging up some junk when I started hearing low growls coming from the far end where the old coal bin had been located. I saw nothing.

I started to smell a bad smell, like something foul burning. Then, I heard a scream. I ran toward the stairs and out the back door. My mother and adopted sister ran up the stairs, too, with fear on their faces. Needless to say, the house remained haunted until the day it was torn down about a year ago. Now, there is just an empty lot...the only one on the whole street where nearly all the houses have been renovated and updated. – *Athena S., Indiana*

## The Figure in My Bed

It's been eighteen years since I lived at that address. However, every time I mention it, I feel a lump form in my throat. I was eight when I first encountered the paranormal. I'd feel brushing against my shoulders, unexplained voices and smells (usually cigarette smoke). At the time I lived with my mother and three sisters (me being the youngest). And, of course, they ALL thought I was insane (and still do). Out of all my experiences, I recall one of the major ones. It scared me tremendously.

I had a tendency to lie awake for a while at night and scan the room for what I called at the time "dark people." These figures would appear around the room and do nothing in particular. I didn't fear them. But I SAW THEM. I would smell, listen and look for them before I went to sleep. This particular night I didn't see any, which wasn't odd but unusual.

Sooner or later, I closed my eyes and was snapped awake by one of these dark figures in the bed next to me. Facing me. They'd never gotten this close, and it frightened me. I couldn't move and felt paralyzed. I tried calling to alarm my sister who slept in a bed in that same bedroom, but I couldn't make a sound. I started to panic. This figure was lying there with no expression or movement. I felt like it was watching me menacingly, without blinking, perhaps. It was darker than dark, but I could make out deep eye holes and its mouth rested slightly open. It felt like hours that it stared, as if it were observing my inner thoughts.

I remember laying there with my eyes open, fearful to even breathe until I could see light peeking through the window. I chirped out a noise similar to one by someone who was trying to talk with their mouth closed. The figure inhaled as if it were going to say something but instead seemed to sink into my mattress.

I don't know if I scared it away or if it was done with its torment, but it disappeared. And, since that night, the encounters with these dark figures have become more frequent and more real. I remember wetting myself in fear that night and when I explained it to my mother the next day, she said I had sleep paralysis and nightmares and explained it away medically. I have since become familiar with using pendulums, dowsing, Ouija boards, etc., (responsibly, of course). Although I'm a grown, married woman, I still check under the bed, and I still prefer a small light source at night before I go to sleep – *Morgan C., Virginia*

## Leave the Bones

I went to the Bell Witch Cave in Adams, Tennessee. I was a teenager at the time. Went through the tour. It passes by a little gravesite, among other things. When you get to the end of the cave, there is a pond-type area with blind fish, supposedly. I heard a piano playing and women giggling. When we left, I did something I shouldn't have. I took a small bone from the little gravesite that was inside.

I got home and that night I woke up to being scratched!! What woke me up to begin with was someone hollering at me in my ear!! No one was there. The next day I took it back!! – *Melissa F., Tennessee*

## Beware What Masquerades as a Child

I've had several frightening experiences. One was when I lived in an old brick bungalow in the city. My then husband left me with two little girls, aged four and two. One night I was sleeping, and I heard a voice call, "Mommy." As I turned to look toward the door, I saw a child who I thought was my daughter Michele.

"Michele, go back to bed," I said.

She giggled and ran. Well, I got up and went to the room that Michele shared with her sister. I flipped on the light and heard the most sinister, evil laughter you ever wanted to hear. My daughters were both asleep. – *Maura C.*

## Don't Look Up

I lived in a house where my then-boyfriend claimed he had performed a curse on someone. The house had a dark feeling, but I tried to deal with it. One night, I felt like my deceased best friend was beside the bed. I felt comforted at first, then that feeling changed to absolute terror. I realized that the demon he had used to place the curse was fooling me. The next day, while I was sitting with his son in the living room, he pointed to the ceiling fan and said that there was a little girl sitting on it. Of course, I saw nothing there. Totally freaked me out! – *Miranda D., Tennessee*

## What Did They Contact?

Having played with a Ouija board enough as a kid with my cousins to have a good background on what happens, I was quick at fifteen to use a friend's board with my boyfriend. I asked who we were speaking with, and the board spelled "Satan." I was concerned about my boyfriend, so I thought TO MYSELF, "You can't have him. I love and protect him."

It spelled, "F*** U, Bitch," and then the open windows

slammed shut. We threw it away and I broke up with the guy. A Ouija board is not a toy. – *Elizabeth D.*


## What Lurks at the Tree Line?

I had been staying with my mother and stepfather over a period of a year. They live on a farm in the country equipped with its own cemetery. My mother talked about strange things happening in the house...strange noises, or items of clothing or personal belongings would go missing without explanation.

When I was there I, too, experienced strange events. There was the feeling of dread and of being watched. There were footsteps in the hallway in the middle of the night, and I would oftentimes wake up to see a small child looking out the window or staring at me from the bottom of the bed. The longer I stayed there, the more things began to escalate. Kitchen items started to disappear. Pots and pans, knives. Glasses would spontaneously break. I would often be woken in the middle of the night by what I would describe as being smacked with great force in the middle of my back and would wake up with visible scratches or marks on my body. There was also what sounded like an infant crying off in the nearby woods and the feeling of something very evil just past the trees, attempting to lure me.

I have subsequently moved back to my home and, to my knowledge, events at my mom's house have deescalated but not stopped completely. – *Nathan B., Kentucky*


## Haunted by Tragedy

It all started when I was a kid . . . from the time I had a memory or probably before. My mom, son, and several of Mom's aunts experience things, along with my mom's dad (my papa) from Kentucky. Mom didn't like talking about any of it.

When I rented my first house after my son was born, almost thirty-four years ago, I was painting the upstairs. I kept feeling that someone was there. Hair stood up on the back of my neck, etc. I would even go look in different places. I didn't see anything, so I just told myself I was being a scaredy cat. Well, my boyfriend, who lived with me at the time, kept hearing something walking downstairs at around 11:00 p.m. Then my nephew heard it. Then my mom. I was sitting in the living room, and I heard it.

It's a small town and everyone knows everyone else. The previous owner of the house had been murdered in a bar several years earlier around this time. The whole little town on the Ohio River seems to be haunted. Every place my family, friends or I lived or owned has had different activity. My little cousin was killed by a drunk driver when he was about two years old. I don't remember him; it was before I was born. But at the house he had lived in, at least one person from every family that has lived there has died of a horrible tragedy. Here are ones I know . . . an older gentleman was hit and killed by a bus. One person was in an accident where the car went backward over a hill and the car caught fire. He could not get out. My nephew was murdered at nineteen. They put his body in the middle of a highway and he was run over by a semi. His stepdad was in a fiery crash and later died. Another sixteen-year-old boy was killed in a car crash. The house burned a few years after he got killed. I know there was at least one other person who died in a vehicle accident that lived there. A few others died of overdoses. Or other causes. Most were younger people.

A couple of years before my nephew died, he told us that something had come down the steps and growled at him. At the time we all kind of laughed it off.

I lived in another place in the town, and I can't even describe everything that happened there. Electronics turned on and off, doors swung open. But then it got really bad. My twelve-year-old son would go to his grandma's house across the street while I was at work. He didn't want to go home at all. It progressed there from stuff falling from the ceiling and almost hitting him in head. Things would disappear and then we'd find them again much later. Like a bottle of body lotion. My son found it months after, inside a computer he was working on. These incidences became so bad we finally decided to move.

I found a place a few miles away. We started getting ready to leave in October and it took me until February. Seemed like whatever was in the house was trying to keep us there. And yes, I live about a mile away from it now in a mobile home. I've been here about eleven years. Things don't seem quite as bad as other places but still happen, like in my spare room it sounds like a bunch of glass falling and breaking. It doesn't happen often but when my son was here, he heard it a few times as well. I actually rent from family and one of my cousins had told me about hearing the glass.

Oh, and one more thing, when I was trying to find out what was going on in the other place, something seemed to always mess it up. Like finding a place online telling me about things to try, and when I tried getting back in touch with the place, it would take me to every kind of website except the one I was trying to get to. That was between 2000 and 2004. I would not have believed half of this stuff if it hadn't happened to us. Now there isn't anything I don't believe if someone tells me about paranormal experiences. – *Sandra V.*

## An Infamous House

After I met my husband, I moved from here, in Tennessee, to Pennsylvania. We ended up moving into the Smurls' house in West Pittston, Pennsylvania. I went to bed one night, walked past my kids' room, and saw a tall black shadow standing by their bed. They were uncovered when I saw this. I ran to get my husband. By the time we got back upstairs, they were completely covered up, tucked in, like it never happened. We went to bed.

In the middle of the night, I woke up. I swear to God I was

on the ceiling, screaming for my husband. When I dropped, I went to step toward the bed and got shoved! I got in the bed, hitting him and screaming and he never woke up!! You gotta know this part, he's a light sleeper. He was in the army and went back in within a couple of months of this. I had NO clue about it being the Smurls' house until I told my neighbors what happened. They told me!! Needless to say, we moved out. – *Melissa F., Tennessee*

## A Cold, Dead Arm

I, my now ex-boyfriend, mother and sister finally found a house to rent after looking for what felt like forever in Melbourne, Florida. We moved in around September and all was okay, just some weird feelings here and there. Then, December 25th, our very first Christmas in the house, is when the first big event happened, and a snowman decoration went flying across the room. We all were sitting around watching a movie and were in shock. After that, everything went to hell fast!

One time in particular, the boyfriend and I were sitting in bed talking when my hair got violently pulled. It was terrifying. After that, things would fly off the walls, even my covers got torn off me in the middle of the night. Once, while in the shower, the detachable shower head flew off and nailed me in the face. I went to work with black eyes and scratches. I wasn't sleeping. I was tortured all the time. It was a nightmare.

I had extremely vivid dreams. One was of me sleeping in my bed. Clear as day I could see my room exactly how it was, but I was asleep and knew I was asleep in my dream, wondering how I'm seeing this when everything got freezing cold. I heard someone gasping for air next to me in bed. A cold, limp, dead arm fell onto my chest. I couldn't breathe, couldn't move. Frozen in fear. I snapped out of it, but I think it actually happened. I was freezing and felt a presence in the room with me. I could tell you stories for days about that house. It was awful. I've always been prone to see and hear things others couldn't, but that house is evil.

We finally ended up doing some digging and called in paranormal investigators. They found some compelling evidence. They called the house a couple of days after the investigation and told my mom to get me out of there immediately. The recording picked up multiple voices. One raspy, terrifying voice I'll never forget said, "Kim is a wh**e and deserves what she gets." Another said, "We want the girl."

We had no money and nowhere to go. I had to stay. I was scratched, knocked down and tortured. We found out we weren't the first people to have experiences in that house and a few owners before us were a young couple addicted to drugs, doing drugs in the house and they ended up dying in there. The girl OD'd in her bed, in the bedroom I lived in, shortly after the boyfriend committed suicide in the house. I can't help but feel the hand that fell on me in my "dream" was hers.

There were also reports of demon activity in the home and I believe that 100% after what I went through. More and more things are coming to my memory as I write this. I tried to leave it all behind but something like that stays with you. – *Kimberly C., North Carolina*

## Keeping Them at Bay

I used a Ouija board at fourteen years old, improperly, and it said a demon came through. He said his name was Rick and we made fun of it, but for two years I was tormented. The night I used it, I felt something try coming up through my legs. It stopped at my knees when I started praying. For years after that, I kept bibles and crosses all around my room and slept with a bible wrapped in a blanket.

I had constant nightmares and spirits would come to me. ALWAYS at my doorway. There was a man with a lantern in my dreams that was ALWAYS at my doorway before any other spirits arrived. I would be trying to sleep and see shadows, or I would feel pressure on my bed like someone was sitting there. I was up all night, every night, crying, scared, seeing things.

My closet door would constantly open on its own. I would make it a nightly goal to try to sleep in my room without being scared. Finally, I switched rooms, but it happened in that room as well. Closet doors, my bed moving and shaking, shadows in different corners of the room. One night I was half asleep and looked at the end of my bed. I saw an all-black, like shadow black, woman with no hair and red eyes staring at me. Her arms turned to tentacles, and she appeared on my ceiling crawling toward me. She spun her head all the way around right in my face and I jolted awake.

After two years I finally learned how to control that energy. I'm still messed with a lot but by the Grace of God, seriously, I'm doing a lot better. I still feel that negative energy every once in a while. There were many instances where I felt or saw this energy in different places, but I have learned to control my fear…some days are harder than others. – *Arin D., Arkansas*

## The Thing in the Closet

I lived in a haunted, 250-year-old house, for seven years. Black shadows, phantom odors, broken objects (including a tempered glass casserole lid that shattered while simply stored in a cabinet), full body apparitions. All my kids are sensitive from living in that environment, but my oldest daughter has seen spirits everywhere all her life. It never felt too scary. More like fascinating. A curious side of nature.

I have many stories, but the scariest was in a house in South Carolina. A closet in the back bedroom always felt bad to be in. Like I was intruding and unwelcome. I broke up with my boyfriend and was packing, and I slept in that room one night while preparing to leave. I awoke in absolute terror. I never felt that way before, right out of sleep. I tried to ignore it, turn my back from the closet. It only got worse. I felt absolutely threatened and in danger of something I could not see. I couldn't stop feeling like I needed to run out of that room. I ran right through an incredibly pitch-black area in front of the door. The feeling left as soon as I shut it behind me.

The next day, my psychic daughter saw it. I could tell because she looked over to the now open door and she gasped and ran into her room. She slammed her door. I asked her later if she saw something and if she would draw it for me. It was a tall dark thing with "snakes of energy" shooting out of its head, with long arms and very long skinny fingers...and bright red eyes. Terrifying. – *Kelly R.*

## Grabbed in the Night

When my wife and I moved to Bowling Green, Kentucky, we rented a haunted house for four or five years. We had a few intense experiences.

On Christmas day, we were heading out to visit family and we left a digital recorder in the living room. You can hear a voice whispering as soon as we shut the front door.

While in our bedroom, we would hear footsteps walking back and forth so often we learned to ignore them. While walking through the hallway at night, I could always look out into the dark living room area and get a strong sense someone was there staring back at me.

One day I was home alone and sitting in the living room. I saw a shadow move across the window. It was daytime and looked like someone was walking in front of the window outside. I jumped up as fast as possible and looked out the window. Then I went outside and looked all around. Nothing.

One night, my wife jolted me awake with a quick movement. She said she felt a hand grab her around the ankle while she was asleep. The next morning, she had scratch marks on her neck.

Another night we were woken up by a loud crash in the kitchen. I ran in and my wife followed. A few of the cabinets were wide open and a large pot was on the floor. The only way to get this pot off the hook was to push it up toward the ceiling and lift it off.

Without warning, my wife passed out. She hit the wall before I could catch her and break the fall. – *Derek W.*

# A Murderous Influence

My experience was from when I was investigating in an old polygamist house in Utah with a group that does public investigations. The team lead is a good friend of mine. For privacy reasons, I'll call him V. This experience started when we were standing around in the front room of the house and V walked past me. I glared at him until he was out of sight and thought, "I want to kill you!" Except that thought was not my own as I don't ever think like that and wasn't mad at him or anything. I had no reason to even be mad, let alone want to kill him.

Either later that night or another time we went, (I can't remember which now), we were all sitting in that same room trying to talk to the spirits. V again was sitting opposite of where I was sitting when I started glaring at him again. I was holding my phone and feeling so tense and angry that I was physically trying to bend my phone.

"Someone here doesn't like you," I told him, which is not normal for me. I am not a psychic or sensitive, so I don't pick up on things like that about other people.

"Like someone in this group of people?" he asked.

"No, like it was something or a spirit here that doesn't like you!" I was feeling almost like I wanted to hurt him.

People who know me know I'm not a violent, mean person and I don't act like that. Even when I'm super mad at someone, I don't think about hurting them EVER. I'm pretty sure something there was trying to influence me to say and feel those emotions to get their message. I've gone to several other locations with this group and have never felt that toward him anywhere else. Not even in other rooms of that same house. It was only that one room in that house.

I am typically a skeptic about spirits communicating with the living but that is one experience I can't debunk. I know myself well and how I normally feel, and that was not me. I wasn't sure if I believed others who had stories like this until it happened to me. I told V about it and he, too, thought it was weird because he knows I'm not like that, either. Definitely one of my most strange experiences paranormally. – *Michelle R., Utah*

## Watch Out

This happened in Kansas. When I was a little girl, my mom and we kids would go to some of my mom's friend's houses because they liked to play card and board games. We kids would play outside or in another room. One night, my mom's friend called and had everyone come over because she had a new game that she wanted to play. The new game? Ouija! We were in the room with them and saw everything.

My mom and her friends started playing and were asking questions. It was answering "Yes," "No," and spelling words out. Then, one of my mom's friends asked the board, "Is the person that is speaking to us good or bad?" It must not have liked the question because the table started shaking, the board rose up off the table about two inches and started spinning in circles…and then it flew across the room! No one was touching the table or the Ouija board when it happened! We all screamed and ran out of the house.

My momma has never messed with a Ouija board again and we don't allow one anywhere around us or in our house to this day. – *Melanie M.*

## Ever Vigilant

I have about five different occasions dealing with possible paranormal experiences. Two of them lasted several months. I still get uneasy thinking of them. Don't know how we made it out without physical harm, but emotional is another story.

The only ones who lived in the house (which had two apartments – upstairs and downstairs) were my husband, our ten-month-old son, my sister and me. No one was living in the downstairs apartment at that time.

We would feel someone, or something, crawl into bed with us and actually wake us up.

We heard loud banging footsteps like someone stomping their feet with boots on. Loud banging on the walls. It was so loud that our neighbors across the street could hear it. It always felt like we were being watched and I got strong vibes that something was about to happen.

My sister was in the bathroom getting ready to take a shower. She felt uncomfortable. She got into the shower and started washing her hair when the shower curtain ripped from the rings. We were in the kitchen finishing getting dinner made and setting the table when we heard the noise and went quickly into the bathroom. My sister was crouched down in the tub crying.

Now the bathroom was about twenty-five feet away from the kitchen. And she showered with the bathroom door open since all the activity started. The only ones who lived in the house (which had two apartments – upstairs and downstairs) were my husband, our ten-month-old son, my sister and I. No one was living in the downstairs apartment at the time. We would feel someone, or something, crawl into bed with us and actually wake us up.

We talked with our reverend about everything that was going on in the house. He told us to have one window open about two inches in one room so we could corner whatever was there. We were to get holy water and go through every room, including the attic, make crosses using the holy water on every window, above every door case before entering and to do all the windows in the apartment as well. When we got to the room with the one window opened, we were to put three more crosses on the door casing before going into the room. Shut the door again and put three crosses on the door casing. All this while reciting the Lord's Prayer.

When we got to the room with the opened window, we shut the door and made the three crosses with the holy water, still reciting the Lord's Prayer. That's when all hell broke out. Things were thrown off our dressers, bedside tables, our son's bassinet was knocked over onto its side and there was a loud pounding on the walls. The floor was vibrating. Through all of this we were still reciting the Lord's Prayer, stronger than ever. And then it went silent.

We just stood there.

My husband went over and shut the window. He placed three crosses on the window frame and one big cross on the window. Oh, and our reverend had told us before we started, we had to remove our son from the property, dressed in red, and to place three crosses on him with the holy water. We did and brought him to my mother's house.

After all this was done, it felt like a dark shadow we hadn't known existed was lifted up. It felt so good. We lived in that apartment for eight months before we did anything about it. One, we felt foolish telling anyone. Only the neighbor across the street knew about what was going on. And two, who would believe three young adults?

We stayed another two months before we moved. My sister continued having nightmares at least twice a week and we still had our eyes and ears open. My sister was still taking showers with the bathroom door open, and no one was left alone. Even though it felt good, we kept aware.

That was the worst one. It happened in August 1980 to June 1981. I have another, not as bad, but it still lingers in my mind. This one was in 2005.

In April 2005 we were out ghost hunting. There were nine of us, mostly kids. We were at a church that we had been to several times, and it was around 11:30 at night. My sister (another sister) and I were standing out front but to the right of the church. The kids and two adults were out behind the church with their cameras and recorders.

I was telling my sister that I could not go past the second window (there are three windows on each side of the church), that something stopped me in my tracks. The hair on my arms stood up and felt like electricity was going through me.

She said, "Well, you always sensed and felt things ever since you were a young teen."

Then we heard an owl. We never heard one there before and were talking about the owl and how strange that was. We'd never heard it any of the times we had been at that church.

Next, we heard a dog bark farther away from the church. Other dogs joined in, and it sounded like they were getting closer. I told my sister to round everyone up because the dogs were getting louder and closer. She brought everyone to the front of the church.

I said, "Don't run, but get into the cars *now*."

Of course, the kids ran. We got into the cars and drove down the road onto a gravel area and got out. The kids started asking why we had to leave so quickly as they were only dogs. I told them it wasn't what I heard, but what I didn't hear. I didn't hear leaves crunching or paws hitting the ground.

We got back into our cars and drove slowly past the church. There was not one dog in the churchyard or driveway. And you know dogs always sniff around.

My sister has never gone ghost hunting again. She told me evil was lurking there and she felt that something attached itself to me, that I was considered the evil's enemy because I was "the warner."

I went back to the church by myself again around 11:30 at night to face whatever was there or whoever was attached to me, to rid it from myself. Since then, I have also had a cleansing and I meditate. Things are okay, although I still have things happen around me. But that's a different story. – *Belinda M.*

# Of Dolls and Ouija Boards

It all started when I was a child. I received a cabbage patch doll for Christmas one year. When I was older, my roommates hated that doll with a passion. They, or I, would set the doll in a certain place every night and, by the next morning, the doll would be moved. We blamed each other until one night we all stayed up. None of us moved the doll but as we watched, it moved from one place to another on its own. That was the beginning.

As I got older, I heard about a place where I lived, so we went out to it. It was there I could hear voices and see shadows. After that I could feel and sense even more things the older I got, and I found out it runs in my family.

My dad had a Ouija board that my friends found. I was in the kitchen cooking when they started playing with it. I didn't know they had until I heard someone scream, "Don't!" I went to the living room and grabbed it, putting it up. They thought it was a game until things went flying off the shelves and knocking and growling was heard. I didn't know how to close it or anything…and, needless to say, that apartment was still active as of ten years ago. I haven't been back.

I can sense things in my house. I can hear them, and I have also seen them. The first time scared me nearly to death. It was night, and I was alone. Everything was black, but this was darker than that. I ran to the bathroom to turn on the light to see if I was actually seeing what I thought I saw. It didn't seem to be evil but scared me. It's still in the house and I can hear it. I am leery of being in the dark, having all the lights off. I need to have night lights around.

One night I was sleeping and woke up out of the blue. I saw a bright ball of light going around my room. I woke my husband and asked him if he could see it. Of course, he doesn't believe in all that. It came to my side of the bed and pronounced my name correctly several times and stayed there…it seems like minutes. It finally disappeared.

The next morning, I called my family to ask who had passed away.

"No one."

Two hours later I received a call that a family member had passed away. They wanted to know how I knew...and let me know that sensitivities run on this side of the family.

I have also captured spirits on night-vision cameras and dream of things before they happen. I have had good and bad experiences and imagine I always will. – *Laura, Oklahoma*

## A Man Possessed

I've had experiences since I was a child. But one chilling string of paranormal events led to me leave my high school sweetheart.

It all started on one of the beautiful Hawaiian Islands. We moved to off-post military housing after his first deployment. I instantly felt something lurking in the shadows. When sitting in the living room alone, I would see shadows moving from one side of the kitchen to the other. The living room and kitchen were separated by a wall, and you could enter the kitchen on either side of that wall. I always tried to rule out what it could be versus going straight to a paranormal explanation. I was always catching something moving out of the corner of my eye and would get weird feelings when I walked into the kitchen or into the laundry room. You had to enter the kitchen to get to the laundry room.

I had been living at the house for about two months prior to my now ex-husband getting back from deployment. I wanted everything set up and perfect. We had been together since the age of fifteen, and never had any major fights. We were the perfect couple that everyone wanted to be.

Things changed fast, soon after his return. I believe it was something darker in that house. No one will be able to convince me otherwise. It started with a BBQ. He was higher up, and we would invite the younger soldiers over during holidays, so they were not alone. At this BBQ, something switched in his personality. He started yelling at me in front of everyone. Pinned me up against a wall. This was the first time he put his hands on me. Another officer sent everyone home. He claimed he didn't remember what happened. I brushed it off even though I was very hurt and confused. This was the first of years of abuse that I endured.

One night, I was sitting on the couch alone and again was seeing a figure walking around in the kitchen. I decided it was time for bed. Maybe I was just really tired, so I ignored it. I started to walk up the stairs. Suddenly, all the hair on my body stood up. I felt a static charge in the air. This is how I know something is around me…which still happens. I kept going and got to the landing. I still had to turn and go up a few more stairs. As I turned right to go up the second set, I looked up.

What I saw, I still remember clear as day when I think about that moment. There was a seven-foot tall, all black figure standing at the top of the stairs. There is a window at the top right of the hall, so I know it was not a shadow being cast from outside. I was struck with fear. I was so scared that the only thing I could do was take a few steps backward and put my back against the wall. I didn't want anything coming from behind me. I stared at it.

It felt like minutes but, in reality, it was probably no more than thirty seconds. I don't know, really. Then, it disappeared. I was hesitant but I went up. I was shocked when I entered my bedroom. My ex was dead asleep, but he had his arm stretched out like he was reaching for something. I did not want to wake him. You know, waking a soldier up a few months after a deployment. I just got into bed. I don't know how I fell asleep; my heart was racing. But the rest didn't last. Something touched my foot and woke me. A figure was standing at the foot of my bed.

In total fear I did what I would do as a child when something visited in the late hours of the night. Obviously, I threw the blankets over my head. Closed my eyes tight. And, eventually, fell asleep.

The next morning when I woke, I had a busted lip. The violence built until we moved. On our last day in the house, I was cleaning. All furniture was out, and I was doing last minute cleaning. My ex was outside in the garage with our neighbors. I was in the living room. I saw a full, clear as day ghost…not see-through at all. It was in the kitchen, and it looked like she came from the laundry room. She was about 5'5" with beautiful brown hair that reached past her knees. She was topless and had a grass skirt on. She looked directly at me, smiled, and walked through the sliding glass, back door on the left side of the kitchen. I ran to the kitchen. Nothing. I ran out in front of all the neighbors still standing with my ex. I didn't mention it to anyone, and we left. Off to our newly purchased house.

Within the first week there, another sighting. Did this darker entity follow us? I think so. We were in bed and my Pitbull puppy was in his kennel outside of our bedroom, in the living room. I was almost asleep. All of a sudden, my phone on the nightstand lit up. It glowed so brightly it lit the whole room. Unusual but whatever. Then I saw it. The seven-foot-tall figure. It moved from the left side of the room. It was so solid, I thought we had an intruder. I watched this figure walk from left to right and then out the door. My poor puppy, still locked up, started whimpering. I never heard him make that noise before.

My ex and I jumped up only to glimpse it glide across the house and into the second bedroom. We turned on every light and ran to the room again, still thinking it was an intruder. Nothing. He started to get fits of rage and anger but never seemed to remember b.s. Physical and mental abuse were constant. My last straw would come. Our last fight was pretty ugly. He rushed me. But this time I looked into his eyes. What I saw frightened me so much that I packed a suitcase for myself and my two daughters and left.

His eyes were completely black. No white could be seen. What was I looking at…my husband? Or some demonic entity taking him over? Raw anger, pitch black eyes, spewing the most offensive language at me.

I left. Took my daughters, moved into a domestic violence shelter and filed for divorce. It was granted in 2013, a year after leaving. I have full legal and parental custody of our two daughters with no contact allowed via court order.

I've been able to see and sense things around me since I was young, and my last paranormal experience was just a few days ago. But that shook me. It broke our marriage. I always question – was he influenced by this dark entity? – *Jennifer K., Alaska*

## With Glowing Red Eyes

My name is Haley, and I was born and grew up in Dayton, Ohio. I've also lived in the same house since I was a year old. Many strange things have happened in those thirty-four years.

I've had sleep paralysis ever since I can remember. I've only experienced it fully in our house. As a child, it was disturbing enough, waking up frozen, only able to move my eyes. Being so young, I always thought it was a bad dream. This came along with seeing countless shadow figures, hearing footsteps and knocks, electronics acting bizarre. I never really felt scared and accepted our "roommate."

Several years ago, something shifted in the energy of our home. One October morning, I went to my room to take a nap before my shift at work that evening. I settled into bed, put my sleep mask on and soon began to drift off. But before I was fully asleep, that familiar feeling came over me. I couldn't move, and, even with my eyes closed, I could see everything in the room as it actually was – only something was off.

In the corner I was facing, just above the doorway to enter my room, a huge black smoky mass came to life. The ominous cloud began to drift toward my bedside and its shape shifted into a human-like form. Before I knew what was happening, this black as night figure stood menacingly over me, its glowing red eyes fixed on my frozen, helpless body. It stood over me with a smile from ear to ear, its mouth full of jagged, dagger-like teeth. Its flesh had a leather, burnt coal look to it as if then and there it had transported from the depths of hell.

I couldn't even breathe, let alone scream. Our eyes transfixed on each other. I began to pray in my mind and think about God. Within seconds, it loosened its grip, and I was able to move and fall asleep. (I don't know how, in retrospect). As I later went to work and got on about my day, I just couldn't help but think about it and I concluded this was no dream. It was very real. And nothing of this earth.

I've only told this to a couple of people, as I know it sounds insane. But it was real, and definitely happened. I can't say if this entity has a name or what it was, but I pray I never see it again in my life. I haven't slept in that room since. – *Haley B., Ohio*

Sometimes the things that scare us are only an attempt at communication... a knock on the wall, a touch, a scent.

But sometimes they are much more.

Be cautious with the unknown, my friends.
Stay safe.

# ABOUT THE AUTHOR

Barb Shadow is a paranormal investigator and researcher, living with her family on the East Coast. She founded the Sullivan Paranormal Society, an investigative team in upstate New York, and has appeared on numerous radio shows to discuss her experiences. Barb has kept a journal of her ghostly encounters for the last thirty years.

Barb's horror series, From the Darkness, began as a challenge to write a novel in a month. With the first draft penned, Barb won the challenge, combining her flair for storytelling with her passion for the paranormal. The series caught fire. Her readers have said they read with the lights on and only when they're not alone. When not writing spine-tingling tales, you can find Barb with headphones on, listening for EVPs from her team's latest investigations.

To find out more about Barb and get updates on her upcoming titles, visit **barbshadow.com**. There you can follow her blog on the paranormal and contact her with any comments or questions you have. She is always happy to connect with fans and those interested in the unexplained.

You can find her team's Facebook page at Sullivan Paranormal Society (and listen to some of the amazing EVPs they've recorded). Not for the faint of heart!

Barb can also be found on Instagram at **barbshadowwrites**.

If you've had a paranormal experience and would like to share it with Barb or have it considered for inclusion in her upcoming anthology, *True Ghost Stories and Hauntings, vol. 2,* you can submit it on the From the Shadows Publishing website, **fromtheshadowspublishing.com**.